Aglaia's Story

Aglaia's Story

Yvonne Pastolove

DENVER, COLORADO

Outskirts Press, Inc.
http://www.outskirtspress.com

ISBN: 978-1-4787-6656-8

Outskirts Press and the "OP" logo are trademarks belonging to Outskirts Press, Inc.

PRINTED IN THE UNITED STATES OF AMERICA

Table of Contents

Chapter 1

L et me start at what I used to think was the beginning. In Geneva spring has arrived unusually early this year, 1864. I am sitting in a classroom and instead of paying attention to the lesson I count the days until I can be on my way home, home being a small town by the name of Brig, in the Valais canton. Valais is a long, narrow valley in Southwestern Switzerland, carved out eons ago by glaciers between two mountain ranges.

I believe that Brig has a perfectly good school for girls although it is small. Unfortunately my father is of a different opinion and insists that I spend four years here, at Madame Verret's 'exclusive' Boarding School. Exclusive, I suppose, because the girls are from places like London, Madrid and Vienna. I like most of them - especially the Austrian twins Ingrid and Veronika who are two years older; they regale us with captivating stories about where they have been and what they'd much rather do than studying! I also have friends among the other girls, but there are a few who pronounce "Brig" with a question mark attached to it and make it sound as if it was a disease - I am not imagining this. They never tire of teasing me about my name and my shoes. It is true that I have yet to encounter another Aglaia, but my name will not surprise you once you know that my parents used to read stories from Greek mythology to me, along with "Sleeping Beauty" and other fairy tales. But more about that later.

On that particular Friday morning we are twenty seventeen-year old girls trying to survive Monsieur Broussard's history class. His lessons are best described as sleep-inducing; I am not the only girl yawning and losing her fight to stay awake. Even my best friend Monique with whom I share a bedroom is struggling. Linette is another good friend. She was kept on as servant after her Great Aunt, her only family, died owing school fees (which tells you something about Madame, doesn't it?), but we have to be careful. "My young ladies are not to be on familiar terms with employees" is one of Madame's cardinal rules. Although strictly enforced, there are ways around it.

While Monsieur Broussard drones on about an English war sunlight streams through the windows and slants across our desks. The tiny bright-green leaves of the trees in the courtyard turn into beckoning fingers and I am seized with the most intense longing to be home. Home with Father and Olga and Simon and my dog Barry. When Father brought the puppy home to me, I had just finished reading a story about the Saint

Bernard dogs that live with the monks up in the Simplon Pass Hospice and, working in pairs, are trained to find and save people lost in the snow. There is always a dog named Barry among them. Naturally that was the name I chose for my dog.

My eyes are closing, all my favorite places are conjured up – I can almost smell newly mowed grass and the honeysuckle behind our house and see the apricot tree in bloom, although it is still too early for that; there might still be some snow on the ground, this being early April.

"Mademoiselle Andereggen, how soon will it be convenient for you to rejoin the class? Perhaps even to answer my question, or is that too much to hope for?"

Monsieur Broussard's sarcastic voice erases the beautiful pictures of home. I steal a quick glance at my friend. She mouths the answer behind her hand, but I have no idea what she is trying to say; I am not good at reading lips and I don't remember the question.

With an expression of martyred patience the teacher repeats, "Mademoiselle, tell us: where and when was the decisive battle fought?"

Battle?

At this very moment I am saved, if only temporarily, by a knock at the door. While the girl sitting closest to the door rushes to open it, Monique quickly scribbles something on a piece of paper and passes it to me under the table. I take it without looking at it - I am more interested in who is at the door and why. This has never happened before. Monsieur Broussard does not tolerate interruptions to his lessons. Never. Under no circumstances. No exceptions.

Linette stands there, looking down at her feet and quickly says, "Beg pardon Monsieur, but Mademoiselle Andereggen is to come to Madame's study immediately." She curtsies, throws a commiserating smile my way and is gone before Monsieur Broussard has regained the power of speech.

When he finds his voice again he doesn't bother to hide his irritation. "Your hearing seems to be particularly impaired today, Mademoiselle. Not waiting for a written invitation, are you? Go! Now! Go!"

He doesn't have to tell me again, but I am very uneasy when I hurry down the stairs and along the hallway towards Madame Verret's study. Something must be wrong, but I cannot think what it could be. I take a deep, scared breath before I knock on her door.

It is opened by Mr. Thornton, our English teacher. He waves me inside. Here I might as well admit that I dislike him, initially because he made no secret of the fact that he considers teaching us the language and works of Milton and Shakespeare far below his dignity. That would have been reason enough, but suddenly, in his second year at my school, he began to stare and get close to me in a way that made me feel uncomfortable. I am pretty but not beautiful - why not stare at Veronica and Ingrid, the Austrian twins instead? They are beautiful. He kept getting too close, but I was convinced that complaining to Madame would land *me* in trouble, not him; they are close friends, exceptionally close friends if you believe the rumors. It took me weeks to realize that all he was trying to do was get a close look at the *locket* I had only recently started to wear every day! I turned around right then and there and quickly tucked it into my blouse, and that is how I have worn it ever since. I don't know what he found so interesting about a gold locket that has small gold circles on a black marble background. Yes, it is pretty and an antique, but that's all there is to it. What I mean is that it is bad enough being summoned into Madame's presence without having him there, too!

As I step into the room I notice that Madame's Nyon chocolate pot and matching no-handle-cups and saucers have been placed on her desk. That is a treat reserved for special rewards, and while I am not aware of having broken any rules lately, I am equally sure that I have not done anything deserving of a reward.

"Sit down, my dear," Madame Verret says in the honeyed tones she reserves for important pupils, meaning girls whose parents are wealthy or well-connected or both. Here it should be noted that this is my first 'my dear' in over three years!

"I am afraid I have some unfortunate news for you," she continues, sitting ramrod straight the way she always does, even when she caresses her cat. She smiles, but her smiles only stretch her thin lips and never reach her eyes.

"It concerns your father," she continues, "He ... ."

I jump from my chair. "What about Father?" I shout. "Has something happened to him?"

"Comportment, Mademoiselle, comportment. Do not interrupt your elders and control your voice." Her voice drips censure as she slowly withdraws an envelope from her desk drawer. Turning it between her hands she at last looks at me. "This arrived by special messenger."

'Special messenger' worries me. Father sends all his letters by regular post. But she didn't say he wrote it, I remind myself, she said it concerns him. I reach over the desk, grab the envelope from her and immediately recognize Simon's slanted handwriting.

Dear Madame Verret,

I am taking the liberty of addressing this to you rather than to Aglaia, trusting that you will be of comfort and help to her when you give her the news.

After visiting the day's last patients, Doctor Andereggen failed to return home this past Monday. I am afraid it may have been hours after he was thrown from his horse before we found him. Everything is being done to make him comfortable, but it is important that Aglaia return home as soon as possible.

With my thanks for your assistance, I am

Sincerely,

Simon Riedmatten

Suddenly weak-kneed, I sit down.

Father had an accident. On Monday. But ... but today is Friday! I take another look and see the letter is dated Tuesday morning; if it was sent by special messenger it arrived here the same day. She kept it from me for *three* days, three entire days, even though Simon wrote to come home as soon as possible - but what immediately worries me even more is that I cannot imagine Father having an accident. He has never had what he calls 'an involuntary dismount'. Besides, his Ajax is steady on any terrain, in any weather, safe and sure-footed even in knee-deep snow. Ajax is also so unspookable that Father used to joke he ought to have named him Adrastos which, he said, means 'not inclined to run away' in Greek. Father knows every road, every path in and around Brig and the neighboring villages, and even though he has amazing vision in the dark, he always carries a small miner's lamp with him, 'just in case'. He is an excellent rider, he never takes chances. What could have happened? Jumbled at first, my thoughts crystallize into the urgent need to rush home. I start to get out of the chair.

"There, there, my dear." Madame pours steaming chocolate into the cups and slides one towards me. "Sit down and drink this, it will calm you. Then we shall discuss how best to handle the situation."

"Yes, do you have some," Mr. Thornton echoes her. He tries to put a cup into my hand, but I don't take it.

"No, thank you. I must go." I sneak at look at Madame's wall clock. If I hurry I can catch the morning coach to Brig. Of course one of those new trains running from Geneva to Lausanne would be faster, but how safe are they? I don't know anybody who has traveled by train. I am also not sure where the station is, most likely a train ticket costs much more than coach fare and I have already spent about a third of this month's allowance - dear God, there just has to be space on the coach ... light-headed and afraid, I know one thing only: I cannot afford to waste time, I must go home. I rush towards the door.

Madame tries to stop me. "I am so sorry, my dear, but I cannot spare someone to accompany you today", she says. "Traveling alone, unaccompanied, that is out of the question for my young ladies. I am surprised you have forgotten. It is clearly stated in our house rules."

Well, *she* seems to have forgotten that I break that rule regularly by traveling back and forth to Geneva by myself. One more 'my dear' in that falsely solicitous, honeyed voice - never mind, I don't have time to listen to her objections. I am going home.

"Wait!" Mr. Thornton follows me to the door and has the nerve to bar my way, saying, "You heard Madame. Go sit down."

"Yes, my dear, we'll all have some chocolate together. That will calm you, my dear."

I wish I could shout at them that I am calm enough, thank you, that the only thing that will make me lose that calm *and* my manners is if they keep pushing chocolate on me which I do not want and if I am called 'my dear' one more time! I square my shoulders and with all the firmness I can muster announce, "I am going now." I manage to push the door open.

"Madame wants you to remain here!" Mr. Thornton barks out the command, muscles it shut again and has the nerve to stand in front of it, arms crossed against his chest, looking ready to do battle. Why on earth does it matter to him whether I leave or not?

Then something extraordinary happens. With a sigh that sounds almost like a sob Madame says, "No, I cannot do this, Anthony, I cannot. Let her go!" Forgetting all about posture she bends forward, covers her face with both hands and weeps - she, to whom comportment and impeccable manners are everything, has called a teacher by his first name and weeps *in the presence of one of her students?* Looking up and seeing that he is still barring my way she shouts at him to let me go. His face mottles into an angry red, he looks ready to burst with frustration. I squeeze by him and hurry out of the room.

I don't understand what it is she cannot do, but that doesn't matter; letting me go is the first decent thing she has ever done for me. I race upstairs to my room. Linette is already there, holding my travel satchel.

"I listened at the door and ran up the back stairs," she says, still a little out of breath. "Of course you must go home. I'll help you pack."

I throw some of my belongings on my bed and she folds and packs them into my bag. What else? Linette points to my morning slippers. Of course. I exchange them for the sturdy walking boots, source of continuous merriment for some of the girls. Coat, bonnet ... what else? A note for Monique. I write it on the back of the paper she had slipped me in class, promise to explain all in a letter as soon as I can. I'll tuck it under her pillow before I leave. Anything else?

"Money!" Linette suggests. Of course! I grab what there is from the various hiding places and stow it in my pockets. I also want to retrieve Simon's letter and remember having dropped it.

After a quick thank you hug to Linette I run downstairs

and listen at the door to the study. All seems quiet. The study is indeed empty and the letter is where I thought it would be, on the floor close to Madame's desk. When I bend down to pick it up I see her cat, busily lapping chocolate from several broken cup pieces and his paws. 'Madame is going to be madder than a wet hen when she sees that broken porcelain!' goes through my mind as I take a quick look at the clock. I have to hurry.

When I leave the study I hear angry voices, Madame's and Mr. Thornton's, coming from the teachers' salon down the hall. Madame's voice has lost its genteel timbre and sounds common and shrill - no, frightened is a better word. And how dare Mr. Thornton shout such ugly, threatening things at his employer! Well, it is nothing to do with me, let them battle it out.

I tip-toe, then run out of the school building. The big iron gates are open and soon I am hurrying down the busy streets, trying not to knock into people with my satchel. I reach the Rues des Alpes, and now it is only a few more streets to the Hôtel de la Poste where the coaches leave from. What if there is no space on the Brig coach - no, I won't let myself think that!

Chapter ||

By the time I arrive at the booking office, I have to catch my breath before I can request passage to Brig.

"One inside seat?" the ticket agent repeats.

I cross my fingers and nod.

"Just got a window seat cancellation. Seats ought to be reserved well in time," he admonishes severely as he hands over ticket and receipt. Frowning, he adds, "Don't know 'bout today's weather; I bet we're in for some rain, I feel it in me bones! Coach'll be leavin' in ten minutes or so."

Hoping that his bones are sending out erroneous messages I watch my bag being stowed and how the driver fortifies himself from a bottle. The other passengers, three elderly ladies and two gentlemen, are already seated when I climb aboard and claim my window seat which, I am relieved to see, faces forward. The guard closes both doors, gives the windows a perfunctory wipe with the usual dirty cloth and pulls up the ladder. He swings himself up on the rear seat, the driver cracks his whip and we are on our way.

I lean back into my corner, close my eyes and try to shut out all the sounds around me. If only I had stayed home. If only I had never gone to that school. The three years I have already spent there have been tolerable only because of Monique and Linette and a handful of other friends, but Father, usually so reasonable, insisted on that fourth and final year. After several discussions during which I had held on to my temper with great difficulty, he had repeated, "It's only one more year, and it may be important that you be fluent in English."

I couldn't help myself and had asked in an almost-shout, "Why? What makes English so important? Nobody in Brig speaks English except you and Uncle Kaspar. And Simon, of course. Well, perhaps the owner of the Post Hotel does, too, but that's everybody!"

"True, true – but nevertheless, I owe it to you, and some day when you ..."

"Some day when I am older I'll understand?" I finished the sentence for him. "Adults always say that, but I'll never understand this. I'll be living right here, in Brig, speaking German and French, maybe a little Italian, that's all I need. I don't care a row of beans about knowing more English!"

Shaking his head at the 'row of beans' but still listening, he methodically replenished items in his medical bag, and when he snapped it shut and stood, I knew our conversation had come to its end and that he was on his way out. He said that we'd be talking about this again soon. Many of our conversations end like this – patients come first, not always but often enough.

When I was small and did not understand why, I would run up to my room, sulk and wait for my mother to come looking for me. She'd sit me on her lap and try to explain Father's dedication to his work. When I'd say that I wanted to be a doctor, too, and visit patients with him, she always said, "Hold on to that dream until you are a little older, sweetheart, then we'll see." She would coax me out of my self-pitying mood with the promise of a game or a story or walk to one of the upper meadows where we'd gather wild flowers. I still miss her very much.

And I did hold on to that dream. I had just turned fourteen when I decided I had waited long enough. I thought about it some more, so I would not be told, as happened sometimes, that I hadn't given the matter sufficient thought. I laid out my plans for Father. He listened patiently and asked, "Sit next to me?"

"Of course! Don't you think it's a wonderful idea?" I asked, nestling into his arm.

"Yes, I do. Believe me, there is nothing that would please me more. It would indeed be wonderful if ..."

That made me sit up. "Why did you say it would be *if*? If what?"

"What I mean is there are problems with your idea that you are not aware of, cannot be aware of." He asked me to wait with my questions until he had laid out the facts for me.

Well, the facts were that women, no matter how intelligent and how qualified, were not admitted to study medicine anywhere in Europe. Why? Because they are women, period. However, he had recently learned that Zurich University, after lengthy deliberations, was getting ready to make an exception in the case of the brilliant young Russian scientist Nadezha Souslova ..."

I forgot about saving my questions and burst out: "Why not? I don't understand. Why can't women be doctors?"

"You cannot study medicine without the proper foundation," he explained patiently. "Girls are not taught mathematics and science in school like the boys are, which makes ours a very short-sighted system; that's why you are receiving some tutoring in these subjects. Your school is the only one that offers some science to girls." He smiled. "I had an idea that someday we might be discussing this, and I've known for a long time that you like science better than memorizing historical dates. But there are other requirements, years of Latin for instance. And even if you acquitted yourself admirably in *all* subjects, the fact remains that elderly men who are opposed to female medical students sit on the admission boards. They cling to the old - we might as well say 'odd' - notions that women 'by their very nature' are not suited for medicine, that 'their innate sensitivity' presents an obstacle, that they have neither the intelligence nor the stamina or strength of men - I know, I know, all of this is nonsense: you'd think someone would point out to them that nurses lift heavy patients every day! The most ridiculous objection, put forth in all seriousness, is that women cannot get close to patients when they are 'expecting' - how about portly male doctors: *can they?* - but as you can see these gentlemen cannot even bring themselves to use the word pregnant! Well, such is today's sorry state of affairs, Aglaia, but it will change in time."

"When? A hundred years from now?"

"No, not in a hundred years," he said, still patient. "When Nadezha Souslova is admitted, other universities - Paris, Berlin, Rome and others - will follow. They are simply waiting for someone to take that first step. Change will come, but I'm afraid not soon enough for you. It will be different for your daughters and granddaughters, you'll see. Meanwhile, you might consider ..."

"No! You know I don't want to be a nurse. Besides, I'm only fourteen – why should I think about daughters and granddaughters? How do you know I want to be married, ever?" My voice squeaked in outrage. What I really wanted to say was "What about what I want *now?*" I like math and don't mind chemistry, at least the little that Madame Verret makes available for a few of her students, but I am not brilliant and I am not Russian; I am from a small town, population less than two thousand, that nobody outside of Switzerland has ever heard of. What chance will I have? "It is not fair!" I wailed.

Father agreed. "No, it isn't, especially if one remembers that the ancient Egyptians had female physicians! There was also a woman doctor in Athens at that time, although she was limited to midwifery and had to wear men's clothing, I believe. Her name ... well, her name escapes me at the moment. I'll have to look it up."

I had stopped listening after 'midwifery'. Father never misses an opportunity to expound on some aspect or another of a conversation, a very annoying habit of his. To be fair, he really has no other bad habits, but I do wonder how he found out about this Nadezha person? I would never doubt his word, but I like to make sure.

"One of my friends from medical school stayed on in Zurich; I had a letter from him just the other day," he explained readily. "He teaches there now."

That in turn sets me to wondering: Father would have made an excellent teacher – does he ever regret returning to Brig and living the life of a busy country doctor? Who sometimes is paid in carpentry or masonry work, firewood, a side of bacon, chickens, a dozen eggs? Or a puppy, that's how I got Barry. It is a quick thought only, because all I really care about is that my dream had collapsed.

My thoughts return to Simon's letter. Why didn't he write in more detail? Where exactly was Father found, how badly injured is he? Brig is in the mountains and it is not unusual for early April nights to be cold, sometimes to dip down towards freezing. Father has never had an accident riding ... what could have caused his fall? Was he suddenly taken ill, had some sort of seizure? I cannot rid myself of the image of Father lying injured and helpless on snowy frozen ground ...

I must have dozed for a while. When I wake up I am not sure where we are but sense that we are moving at a good speed. Even with changes for fresh horses we should arrive in Brig before nightfall – if the weather holds, if the coach doesn't throw a wheel, if the driver remains sober ... *if* all these 'ifs' line up, then Geneva-Brig is one day's coach journey. I pray silently that nothing may delay us.

After Montreux the road is rougher, and now the afternoon sun disappears behind big grey clouds. The gentlemen leave the coach at the next stop, Martigny, which is where the Rhône makes that ninety- degree turn and heads north towards Lake Geneva. They have to hold on to their hats; a strong wind whips their coats. I know that means a storm might be brewing up ahead somewhere. We make it past Sion's twin peaks, with their medieval castle or church on top, and have just climbed up to the next village, Visp, when the coach lurches and comes to a jarring halt. One of our horses whinnies, in pain, I think. The ladies clutch at each other and scream, "Oh Lord, we are going to go over!"

I wrestle the coach door open, jump down and notice that one of the horses has indeed pulled up lame. The driver comes around, takes a quick look, scratches his head and shrugs, "Ladies, this is it for the day. You will be escorted to the Inn; they always have rooms. It's only a few steps, luggage will be brought to you. This way, if you please."

"Can't we get another horse?" I plead.

He shakes his head. "Not today we can't. Look at that sky, bet it pours 'fore you know it. Ever see what happens to this road in a big rain, with some snow still piled up on both sides, huh?"

"Of course I have, but ..."

"No buts about it, little lady. We continue in the mornin'. *If* we can."

That leaves me only one choice. "In that case," I ask him, "could you have my bag delivered to Brig, to the doctor's house? It's at the edge of town; everybody can point it out to you. Of course you will be paid for your trouble."

"What did you say?" He looks at me as if I had spoken to him in Swahili. I repeat my request, more slowly, explain that it is important I get to Brig *today*, that I have grown up around here and know the roads."

"You're not aimin' to go on, on foot? To Brig? Don't mind me sayin' so, that is a terrible bad idea. Terrible bad. Rain's comin' for sure, and it'll be dark afore you know it."

"Will you take my bag, please?"

He throws up his hands and mutters something under his breath. When I turn to leave, he calls out, "Miss, wait a moment!" He disappears into the Inn and returns carrying a ladies' hooded coat and an umbrella.

"Take these," he says gruffly, still shaking his head, "they got left behind months ago, looks like nobody's goin' to claim 'em. But don't never say I didn't warn you." He hurries inside as the first drops splatter down on the pavement.

I call after him that I would see to it that everything is returned and that he will be paid, shrug into the coat, and pull the hood over my head. I open the umbrella and with shoulders hunched and my head tipped down against the wind I am on my way.

There is something almost hypnotic about rain drumming down on an umbrella. I keep to the main road for what may have been about an hour before stronger, shifting winds keep turning it inside out. Three of the spokes snap, one after the other, and I drop the useless thing by the wayside. Now I have another hand free to hold on to the hood under my chin.

Of course the driver was right. Steadily, the gullies on both sides of the road transform themselves into gushing torrents. Up here the Rhône is little more than a fast-flowing mountain stream, but it floods when the snow melts and also during heavy rains, especially at this time of year. Old people still talk about the bad floods of 1818, and that was nearly fifty years ago.

I know that what on a nice dry afternoon is a pleasant walk of two to three hours will take longer today. I am also thinking it might be wiser to go by the upper path which leads through a forest. There will be more snow up there, but the trees would offer some protection and later it will be an easy half hour downhill to my house. It will be darker in the woods, but I have never been afraid of the dark. Now is not the time to start.

I really feel the cold wetness by the time I leave the main road, but 'nobody melt from water.' That's what Olga always said when I was small and balked at going out in the rain. I start to recite "Kaspar, Melchior and Balthazar" to every four steps as I push uphill, those being not only the names of the three Kings who followed the star to Bethlehem but also the names of the three towers of the Stockalper Palace, Brig's most imposing building: reciting something, or simply counting, helps to keep putting one foot in front of the other ... Once the towers come into view I'll know that I am almost home.

Snow makes walking on the forest path slow going, but when I come out of the trees, the rain has slowed to a drizzle and the thunder has moved farther away. The day's last light is fading, but it lasts long enough to guide me past some familiar landmarks – a logger's hut, the wooden cross where years ago a wanderer had fallen to his death, the fountain, hollowed out from a big tree trunk, now overflowing with rainwater. Down in the distance lights are coming on - I see the outline of Brig's rooftops nestled around the two churches, and here are the three towers! Just in time. I am chilled through and through when I start downhill.

A light is always left burning deep into the night in our house so that people in need of the doctor can find their way easily. When I spot it I break into a run, not that it is much of a run what with my legs leaden and the rest of me hampered by soaked-heavy clothing. Normally I climb over the low stone wall that surrounds the house and garden, but I don't think my legs are up to climbing over anything. At last I am at the gate, wrestle the latch open with cold-clumsy fingers, make it up the three stone steps, grab the brass knocker and pound it against the door, over and over ...

Chapter III

I hear Olga's annoyed, "Comin' comin' fast as legs can!" from inside, punctuated by Barry's excited bark as the door opens. My dog squeezes through, jumps at me, knocks me down and starts licking my face with his usual slobbering exuberance. Olga stands over me, saying, "Saint Jadwiga n' Saint Bystrik! What happen, Child? You bone soak!" Scolding, she drags Barry off me, helps me to my feet and pulls me inside.

"Mercy, look you! What happen?" She peers at me through her wire-rimmed spectacles, but before she can say anything else I wriggle out of her grasp.

"I'm just going to run up and see Father."

"Lookin' like drown cat? Where brains - still outsides?" She peels me out of the water-soaked coat. "Think how you scare poor man! First: off with the wets. After: hot bath!"

"Olga, for God's sake, no! No bath. I want to see Father."

"*Not lookin' like this!* He sleepin'. Doctor Simon say sleep very important." She sits me down on the hall bench. "Sit, no move."

"All right, all right." I give in. Of course I don't want to worry Father. I am sure I look a fright and I still cannot keep my teeth from chattering. Barry has ceased welcoming me and lies happily collapsed at my feet. I let Olga take care of me the way she has all of my life, loving and bossy, comforting and scolding all in the same breath. She helps rubbing me dry after the hot bath, brushes my hair and stands over me while I drink scalding hot honey-tea and eat two slices of her buttered peasant bread. Only then is she satisfied and says, "Now go!"

Father is asleep when I tip-toe into his room. There is a bandage over his left forehead, but his face does not feel hot when I kiss him. I hope that is a good sign and sit down by his bed.

I don't know how much later my eyes become heavy with a drowsiness I don't have to fight. I am home. I let Olga pull me away to my room and tuck me in after she promises several times "I come if change."

When I wake up I cannot tell whether it is still night, or could it be morning already? I run to the window and open the shutters. Morning, late morning! I must have slept for hours instead of seeing Father again, instead of talking to Simon! Why didn't somebody wake me?

I throw on some clothes, run my fingers through my hair and bolt out of my room as Simon is coming out of Father's room. "Why didn't you wake me last night?" I shout at him.

"And a good morning to you, too." Simon takes me by the arm and walks me over to the window seat at the end of the hallway. "Let's sit here and talk for a minute."

"I don't want to sit."

Simon shrugs. "Stand if you like. There are some things you ought to know and there is no easy way to say this: your father has a couple of broken ribs and a head injury, in itself not too alarming, but we can't rule out concussion. His breathing is somewhat labored which is to be expected and he developed a fever earlier this morning. Low-grade so far; still, it's never something we like to see ... we don't know how long he was lying in the snow, exposed to the cold. I hope it doesn't turn into pneumonia." He shrugs tiredly. "Someday there will be more effective medications and treatments for this; for now all I can do is try to keep his fever down. And wait and see ..."

I sit down.

Not that again. Not wait and see again. Seven years ago my mother died of pneumonia after a long illness. Then, too, I had been told to wait and see. This couldn't be happening again. There had been nothing to help her then; was there really *nothing* now, so many years later? Overcome with the most awful feeling of helplessness I lash out at Simon ... why didn't he let me see Father again last night? How can I be certain that he has enough experience, that he knows all there is to know about new treatments? There must be more that he could do. And why did he go out again last night instead of staying here? Who or what is more important than Father?

Stunned, Simon looks at me. He bites back an angry retort, gets up and leaves without saying another word. I watch him go and immediately regret having shouted at him - when Simon is upset or worried or tired he doesn't bother to disguise the slight limp that an accident has left him with. He has been Father's assistant for five years, hired straight out of medical school. In the past he used to treat me with the amused tolerance I assume big brothers show their younger sisters, but he was always my friend. Always.

And I had hoped that he would notice that I am all grown up now ...

The curtains are still drawn when I go into Father's room. He is propped up against two pillows, arms stretched out stiffly on the white comforter. I step closer. His face is moist with perspiration that I am afraid does not come from the heat generated by the room's tile oven. A low-grade fever, Simon had called it, but Father feels warmer than that. A basin of cool water with a small cloth has been placed on the night stand. I dip the cloth into the water, wring it out and carefully dab his face.

"I'm here, Father," I say. "I came as soon as I got Simon's letter."

His eyes open, close again.

"It's me, Aglaia," I repeat, leaning over and kissing his cheek. It feels warmer, too warm.

"Aglaia?" With an effort, he opens his eyes again.

"Yes, Father, I'm here, I came as soon as I heard."

"You are here ... that's good." A smile hovers on his face as he reaches towards me. "Good." His grip is as strong as I remember. Surely that is a good sign.

"I'm glad you are here, so very glad ... there is something I should have told you years ago, but I kept putting it off. Always thought there would be more time, but now ... you must listen, Aglaia, it is very important." He attempts to sit, but gives up and winces.

"Lie still, Father," I beg. "Whatever it is, tell me when you feel better. I am not going away, I'm staying. Tell me later. Tomorrow."

"Yes, tomorrow, and meanwhile take two of these; they'll help you sleep." Unnoticed by me, Simon has come back into the room, carrying a fresh glass of water. He listens to Father's chest, takes his pulse, then gives him the pills and holds the glass for him.

And that's how it is for the next few days. Father wakes for brief moments, and every time he does, his breathing sounds harsher and must have been painful although he tries to hide it. A few times he seems to want to talk and becomes agitated; I manage to calm him by saying we'll talk later, when he feels better. I stay in his room, except when Olga invents an errand for me which requires buying something urgently needed for dinner, for some strange reason available *only* on the other side of town. Of course I know what she is doing, but I am too tired and too worried to argue. Simon looks in on Father often, even late at night, but all he says is 'no real change' or 'fever is slightly elevated'. I don't know what to say to him.

Two mornings later Father's temperature has climbed higher still. Even if Simon had not looked so concerned, I would have been alarmed: this had happened with my mother, too. I tell Olga that she can forget about trying to get me out into the fresh air, that I am not going anywhere. For once she doesn't give me an argument.

Father awakes just before noon. I kiss his cheek which feels much too warm.

"Aglaia?"

"Yes. Are you feeling any better?"

"Of course, now that you are here. I've been waiting to talk to you ..." His voice trails off; he looks worried. "There is something I need to tell you. I should have told you years ago but kept putting it off ... I thought there would be more time, but there may not be ... Aglaia, this is very important."

I am frightened. "Lie still," I beg him, "I am not going away; whatever it is, tell me later, when you are stronger."

"Yes, time for your medication." Unnoticed by me, Simon has come into the room, carrying a glass of water. After he checks his pulse and listens to his chest, he hands Father the pills.

"I'll just sit with him," I announce. This is the second time Simon has interfered when Father wanted to tell me something. Why does he keep doing that?

"No, Aglaia, he needs rest, complete rest." Simon grabs me by the arm. I am so taken aback I let myself be led out of the room. "He needs rest, lots of rest. Just as well I came in when I did. Excitement is not good for him - didn't I warn you not to get him excited? Did you forget?"

"*No, I did not forget!* I didn't do anything to excite him!"

"Well, not deliberately, I know that - but it must have been something you said."

"It was not!"

He doesn't answer, just maneuvers me down the stairs and into the kitchen where Olga has set out lunch. He holds out the chair for me.

"I'm not hungry."

"Suit yourself." Looking annoyed he sits down. As if there was nothing on his mind he finishes his bowl of soup, then helps himself to bread and sliced ham, cheese, hard-boiled eggs and gherkins and begins to eat. He eats very quickly, he always does. In between large bites he announces that he has to leave soon. "So if you still have questions, Aglaia, now is the time to ask. And please sit, I'm getting a stiff neck looking up at you."

How can anyone look so unchanged - same unruly dark hair above the high forehead, same brown eyes behind strong glasses, same kind expression on his face except for new lines of worry and fatigue - and be so different, so cold, so annoying?

"Well?" Simon has finished his wine and leans back in his chair.

I sit and say, "I want to hear about the 'accident again'. With *all* the details this time. Please."

Pushing his empty plate away Simon sighs and answers in a tone that matches mine. "Monday your father was out most of the afternoon. He had mentioned earlier looking in on the Eggers on the way home; there is still scarlet fever around, their youngest has been poorly and what with Martha expecting twins ... well, I wasn't concerned when he wasn't back by supper, you know how often he is asked to stay and share a meal. I finished up in the surgery, went into the library to look up something and lost track of time. When I heard the eleven o'clock bells I realized it was time to go back to my place. I let myself out, saw that it had snowed - that's when I noticed Ajax standing by the barn, saddle still on. There was no sign of your father anywhere."

"And?"

"And, as I've already told you, I ran next door and woke Benedikt and his brother. We took your father's wool muffler along for Barry. First we looked for him at the Egger farm, but they said he had left hours earlier. Your dog insisted on following some horse tracks which led up to the old mill; that's where we found him. He must have taken a bad fall and ..."

"But that's not on the way home from the Eggers at all, that's going the wrong way, in the wrong direction!" Do you know why he went up there?" I interrupt him.

Simon manages a tired smile. "No, I wish I did ... I asked around, the next day, but of course nobody had heard or seen anything, that late at night. I did ask your father, too, but he would only shake his head, just a little, and then he closed his eyes. He made it clear that he will not talk about this."

"I don't understand why not, and I don't understand Father meeting someone up there! You know that he has *never* had 'an involuntary dismount' " - Simon smiles at my use of Father's expression - "and you know how steady Ajax is. Father knows every path, every road around here better than anyone else, in any weather, even in the dark. And he always has that small miner's lamp with him. I cannot understand how this happened." I am close to crying.

Simon nods. "I know, nothing about this makes sense. We never found his lamp ... I was wondering whether he might have fallen asleep ..."

"That's impossible! He wouldn't, not riding!"

"We don't know that, Aglaia, not with any degree of certainty," Simon says reasonably. "It might have happened if he suddenly wasn't feeling well. Or felt disoriented."

"What are you saying? That he was ill and you never bothered to tell me?"

"No, I didn't say he was ill. Tired from working long hours, what with so much illness up and down the valley. I've taken on as much of his patient load as he would let me, but you know how he feels about his patients. He can be quite stubborn – I suppose you get that from him." He smiles the way he always used to smile at me, and just for a moment the old Simon is back. I don't know what to say.

Simon gets up and holds out his hand. "There is nothing more I can tell you. I know how hard this is for you, Aglaia, but please remember that it is hard for all of us. So - still friends?"

"Friends," I agree stiffly.

"Good. Then, as one friend to another: that was brave *and* foolish, the way you got yourself home the other day, walking all that distance, but what is important now is to see that your father takes in plenty of fluids, tea, water, soup, and some soft food, it doesn't much matter what ... and above all, he needs rest. Please: no more excitement. Try to keep him quiet, will you?"

I watch him walk out of the kitchen. When did he become so all-knowing, so all-annoying? Why remind me again, as if I were a thoughtless three-year-old? And again he leaves. When did he develop this habit of never being where he is most needed? How can he be more urgently needed anywhere than right here at home?

I sit down again and realize I am hungry. I am still eating when Olga comes back into the kitchen, carrying my washed and dried clothing.

"Need mendin'," she says disapprovingly, "and here – this in pocket." She hands me Simon's badly smudged letter and a smaller piece of nearly disintegrated paper. My note for Monique - I never put it under her pillow! I can only make out part of a word: 'Tow...?' In a flash it comes to me: the battle of Towton, War of the Roses, red and white, Lancaster and York. According to Monsieur Broussard the bloodiest battle in English history, fought in a snowstorm, fourteen-hundred-something. *Now* I remember these unimportant details? I crumple both papers into a wad and throw them into the fireplace.

Olga beams at me while I finish eating. "Better 'n school foods, hm?"

"Much," I agree.

I help her wash up and put things to right in the kitchen, then I tell her that I am going back up to sit with Father.

She is ahead of me the way she so often is. "I look, he fast sleep. You, I, we sit outsides, sun look cross" which I translate into 'sun peeking through'. We walk out on the porch, she lowers herself into the rocking chair. I sit down on a stool at her feet, the way I always do. A contented Barry stretches out next to me.

"Tell me," she said. "You no make sense. I think maybe I not hear good. Why not say take to door?"

I tell her.

"You walk - from Visp? You no brain girl!"

I nod and shrug at the same time.

"With thunder n' lightnin'? No sense in stubborn head, no sense! What if fall, be hurt?" Her voice rises in anger, but when I look up at her there are tears in her eyes. "Never do again!" she threatens. "Lord, when I think what ..." She pulls me up and gives me a good shake before she holds me so tightly I can hardly breathe.

After a while she says, "Now go ... he not love you more, you not be better daughter not even if you ... oh no, no, no ... idiotá, idiotá, idiotá, oh no!" Looking aghast at what she has let slip, she turns red to the roots of her graying hair, hits the side of her head before she claps both hands in front of her mouth and hurries inside.

I run after her. "Wait, Olga, wait! What do you mean 'I could not have been a better daughter, not even if I ... not even if I what? What, Olga, what? And why did you call yourself an idiot?'"

Her face is red with embarrassment or anger and she waves me away. "Semmi, semmi. Go upstairs, go."

"Stop talking Hungarian to me, you know I don't understand it! What is semmi, and what *did* you mean: '*a better daughter not if I*'? Not if I what? That is what you said, you know you did. Tell me! I have a right to know. Olga, you cannot say that and then walk away as if it was nothing!"

"*Is* nothin'! Semmi be the Hungarian nothin'. Since when you think all words come out silly old woman, they important words?" She looks angry and scared, brushes off more questions and starts to walk away. "Heaven sake, you never say what no mean? Semmi - is nothin', like I already say. Go, go! I have work." She hurries away, mumbling to herself in rapid, sibilant Hungarian. It is what she does when she is upset or angry.

I doubt I'll get anything out of her now, but I am going to get to the bottom of this, I will! It would be too easy, too comforting to believe that she meant nothing. I am convinced there is no chance of that because I know her. I may have just learned that 'semmi' means 'nothing' in Hungarian, but whatever it is, it *cannot* be nothing. Not in any language!

I go upstairs. Father is sleeping.

I sit at his bedside. My thoughts keep revolving around Olga's 'not even if', and if I am certain of one thing it is this: she is not a silly old woman. Far from it. She rarely talks about her life before Brig, but we know that she lost her entire family and a short time later also her new husband Marek, a Hungarian freedom fighter who was killed by the Russians, she told us. She hid out in a forest with other refugees for a long time, never said how she came to Brig, but she firmly believes God's hand guided her to my parents' home. Little by little she learned to understand our dialect which she still speaks with a guttural Hungarian accent and a total disregard for grammar.

My mother taught her to cook local dishes like raclette; she introduced us to Hungarian stuffed cabbage and Kielbasa with dumplings. She grinds poppy seeds the required three times for the tortas she bakes for our birthdays and makes the best apricot jam (and knows that I climb into the tree to get her the juiciest fruit every year). No, she is far from a silly woman, even though she does hold on to some old Hungarian superstitions - such as not doing any work on December 13, like all other decent women, because on that day all the witches come out and do their mischief! She is clever and loyal and has been part of our family for over twenty years. She never keeps her opinions to herself, which can be annoying, but she also never lies. And I am sure she knows things that I am not aware of.

I also don't know what I would have done without her after my mother's death. Father threw himself into his work; there were days when I hardly saw him. Olga took care of me, tried to distract me, put up with my tantrums and outbursts and moodiness, my crying. For months she sat with me every night, telling me all the Hungarian tales she could remember. For weeks I went to sleep with the nameless Princess of the "That is not True" fairy tale who would marry only the young man who could tell her father the King a long story so implausible that he would eventually exclaim, 'That is not true!' - and then she'd hum the lullaby her own mother had sung to her, over and over again, until I was asleep ...

Father is still dozing. I get up and walk around the room. Reminders of my mother are everywhere - her portrait, showing her as the sweet-faced, intense and sometimes inconsolable woman she had been; her toilet articles, hair combs, a small bottle of rose water - I uncap it and with the faint fragrance her memory drifts up stronger for me than it has in many years. There is an unfinished piece of embroidery on a chair by the window – how Father must love her still to keep so much of her in this room. I walk over to the massive armoire and peek inside. It still holds her clothes.

Quietly, I sit down next to him again. He does not look well. When he opens his eyes I offer him a drink, but he only manages a few sips of tea. A new rattling sound in his breathing alarms me.

"I must talk to you, Aglaia," he says suddenly. "Now, not later. You must listen."

Perhaps letting him speak is less upsetting than being put off again. As I debate this with myself he smiles and says, "Suddenly you are all grown up. I know I should have told you all of this long, long ago ... they have been good years, the years we had together, yes?"

"The best, and we'll have many, many more," I answer, trying to keep a growing worry out of my voice.

"There is not enough time to tell you now, but I wrote down the most important things. Promise me ... promise that you will try to understand. I was so certain that I ... that we were doing the right thing at the time. It felt natural, so right - and it made a world of difference to your mother, a world of difference ... "

I don't understand what he is talking about, see only his restlessness.

"You don't have to tell me more now," I tell him, taking his hand. "I promise I'll understand whatever it is. Please don't worry."

It is as if he hadn't heard a word.

"Aglaia, you must look for my notebook. In the library. Not with the medical books, of course, because Simon uses those. With the other books. Promise to find it and read it. It explains everything. Promise?"

"Yes, Father, of course I promise – but Simon told me how important it is for you to rest; we can talk again later ..."

"No, now!" he says and motions to his night table. "There is a key inside that drawer. Take it out. Now."

I reach into the drawer. Behind the spare candles and matches I feel a small key and hold it up to him.

He nods. "Yes, that's the one. After I'm gone ..."

"No! Don't ... "

He silences me with the smallest of gestures and continues. "After you have read the notebook, remember: *after* you've read it, go to the attic. The key fits a small trunk ... I should have talked to you about this a long time ago. I should have, but I ... I always thought there would be enough time to add what I didn't write down earlier. The notebook explains everything ..." His voice is a mere whisper now.

I am trying to hold back tears. He reaches for my hand, presses it and again said, "Promise me, Aglaia?"

"I promise, Father, I promise." I would have promised him anything.

He is exhausted, but also relieved, I see. This must have been very hard for him. I kiss him, careful not to brush up against his poor ribs. He looks like he might fall asleep again, but there is a strange stillness about him, underneath the feverish flush, which frightens me. My mother had looked like this ... Why is Simon *never* around when he is needed?

A little later Olga brings up supper. She doesn't look at me, not once. Father manages only a few sips of broth, and my mind is too full of what he has tried to tell me – the notebook, the key, the trunk in the attic. What has he left for too late? It is not like him to be secretive, so mysterious. Adding that to what Olga has let slip, I become more and more convinced that I have reason to worry. Later she comes back for the trays, still muttering to herself in Hungarian.

Later still, Simon rushes in, and immediately looking alarmed, examines Father and announces that he will spend the night here. I answer that *I* am going to do that. He answers that nothing would be served by two people sitting up all night, that he will come and get me the moment there is a change. I tell him that he can argue until he is blue in the face or until the cows come down from the upper pastures - whichever happens first - I am staying!

Without a word he sits down on the other side of Father's bed.

When I wake up, I think I hear someone calling my name, but I am in my room, still in my clothes, lying on my bed - and immediately I am furious! I don't remember walking out of Father's room because I did not! I run to the door, yank it open and am face to face with Simon.

"Why did you make me sleep in my room ..." That's how far I get before his hand clamps down over my mouth, none too gently, and he says, "Because I caught you before you fell off your chair, that's why! I told you I'd come for you as soon as there is a change."

I tear past him into Father's room. His breathing is shallow and uneven, his eyes closed in an unfamiliarly sharp face, and there is a frightening stillness about him – he is losing the look of the man who has walked in the mountains with me, who taught me to ride and to fish, to swim in one of our lakes whose water is numbingly cold even under a hot August sun. Who read with me. The most cherished and most important person in my life who tried to teach me patience, compassion and kindness and so much more. I am not done learning, I need more time with him ...

Simon whispers something to me.

I brush him aside. I don't need to be told, I know. I kiss Father, sit down by his side and put my hand into his.

Simon keeps watch from the window.

We stay like this for a long time.

Until Simon tells me he is gone.

Chapter IV

The church service is like all services, I suppose. I hardly remember it.

In silence, we file out of the church behind the pall-bearers, Father's friends and neighbors, most of whom he has known since childhood.

Two of my school friends, Vreni and Renate, join us with members of their families; so do women who had been my mother's friends but with whom I had lost touch. I am surprised at the throng of people who stand there, quiet and appropriately solemn, as we pass - but thinking of how much Father had done for so many, it is not surprising.

The cemetery is only a short walk away. Kind people come up to me and murmur kind words, kiss me, pat my shoulder, offer help. But there is no help for this. Their words of sympathy don't reach me.

On the way home I sob into Olga's large supply of handkerchiefs. Red-eyed herself, she immediately bustles about making coffee and setting out plates of food. Then she makes me stand in the living room to accept words of condolence as people file in. I can only nod, my throat is too tight to speak and I cannot bear kind words. I am in a dark place which is getting darker and darker.

I don't know how much later it is when I feel that I can't do this for one more second. I slip out of the room and whistle for Barry. Together we race uphill, towards the Simplon road. Father and I have a special place up there, at the edge of the forest. I need to keep him with me, try to recapture the times we sat up there, our backs against sun-warmed boulders, sharing that special closeness. He would talk to me about life in words I sometimes only half-understood – he told me for instance that the straight and narrow path isn't always the best one to follow because you might miss too much of what is all around you. He talked about how beautiful our valley is, but he also said that it is small and that there is a big world out there. He had studied, practiced and traveled to many interesting places when he was young before he knew who he was and that he wanted to return home. He even told me that, when the time came, he hoped I would fall in love with a young man who would love me not only for my pretty face but also for my quick mind and my kindness, and that he would want me to grow into the woman Father knew I could become ...

Other memories flicker in and out of my mind. Spring flowers are pushing up everywhere. Spring

Gentians, pink and white Rock Jasmine - soon it will be time for the purplish Lady Slippers, Mountain Arnica and Maennertreu, those brown unpretty flowers whose curious name means 'faithful men'. No Edelweiss, they only grow higher up. Father taught me all their names and never tired of telling me the legends of our valley.

Naturally, his favorite legend is also my favorite:

There was once a young shepherd boy whose goats kept running away from him drink at a different spring. One day he stuck a finger into the water, licked it and realized it was salty - small wonder the goats preferred it! Curious, he followed the water into a cave, lost his footing and tumbled down into darkness. When he woke up from what he thought had been a nap, he had grown a beard which reached down to the ground and his hands were the gnarled hands of a very old man. With great difficulty he climbed out of the cave and made his way down to his village where people thought he was a drunken vagrant, what with his wild talk about some angry elves who jealously guarded the secret of their salt caves. At first they made fun of him, but eventually he became such a nuisance that he was threatened with jail. Luckily, a little girl then but now a grandmother with a family of her own, remembered the story about a goatherd cousin who had disappeared decades earlier and took him in. Father used to end the story by saying, "He lived long enough to lead the villagers to the caves and to show them how the elves mined salt. And salt is being mined there to this day – by modern methods, of course!"

Remembering has let some light into the dark place and the silence has wrapped itself around me like balm. I sit until the light cools to blue and the shadows grow longer. One by one lights come on down in the valley. It is time to go back. I receive the expected scolding from Olga for disappearing without a word before she hugs me.

At dinner that night, Simon reminds me that Uncle Kaspar expects both of us in his office, first thing in the morning. He is Father's best friend and lawyer and, although we are not related, has always been Uncle Kaspar to me.

"Can't you go without me?" I ask, without looking up.

"Hardly. You belong there much more than I do." Simon sounds irritated. My question may have been foolish, but all I hear is how the distance between us is growing larger.

In the morning we walk to Uncle Kaspar's office together, if keeping a careful arm's length between us can be called together. I am impatient to get this over with and have to remind myself not to race ahead. We don't talk to each other.

Uncle Kaspar is waiting behind his paper-covered desk and, in the presence of his clerk and another witness, reads Father's will. It is a short and simple document:

House and its contents are left to me, with the exception of the surgery and all the medical books and medical journals which go to Simon provided he agrees to continue practicing medicine out of the house and also takes up residence there. I am charged with continuing to pay Olga's wages, including future raises, whether she leaves my employ or not, and to see to her welfare whether I decide to remain in Brig or not. Whether or not, whether or not ... why would I leave Brig?

With effort I bring my attention back to the proceedings. There are bequests, among them one to the orphanage – I used to accompany Father on his visits there when I was small and bring Olga's special soft cookies to the children. Uncle Kaspar is to administer the estate until my twentieth birthday or my marriage, whichever occurs first, and he is to make available to me any funds necessary for travel abroad. Marriage? Travel abroad? Why did Father think I would want to travel, to marry? I never said that to him. I don't want to go anywhere I think again while Uncle Kaspar reads an addendum which declares all moneys owed to Father forgiven.

How very much like him. I rummage for a handkerchief in my bag and only catch part of a sentence which ends with "well provided for". I am still trying to comprehend why Father thought I might want to travel abroad ...

"Aglaia," Uncle Kaspar repeats patiently, "I know this is difficult for you, but try to understand this: your father has left you very well provided for."

I look up. How is that possible - when Olga was paid late so often because there was not enough money in his desk drawer?

"I don't understand."

"Well, it surprised me, too," he admits. "All I know is your father invested money shortly after you were born. He never discussed details with me, only told me that it was for your future. I have seen the papers: he didn't withdraw one cent for his own use. What this means, Aglaia, is that you have no financial worries – provided you use your inheritance prudently. You are young, and I would be greatly remiss in my duties if I didn't caution you to be careful about how you spend it." He smiles indulgently. "You do have a tendency, sometimes, to act first and think later."

I know, having been told so often enough. I look over at Simon who sits stone-faced, staring straight ahead. I suppose it is asking too much of him to be glad for me.

After that, Uncle Kaspar asks whether I have any questions for him. I say no, not at the moment, thank him and ask him to keep on doing what he had been doing.

We start walking home together, but after a while Simon mentions a patient who lives on the other side of the river and goes off in that direction. True or not? I tell myself that either way it does not matter.

When I tell Olga about the will, relief shows on her face and I realize how worried she must have been about her future. She has no life other than one she shares with us – with me, from now on. Because feeding those in her care is how she deals with problems or emergencies, she sets about preparing my lunch and stands over me while I 'clean plate.' When she says she needs no 'underfeet' help in her kitchen, I decide to go to Father's 'book-lined sanctuary' which is what he used to call his library.

That sounds easy and simple, but I am afraid, truly afraid of what I'll find. I cannot imagine what the notebook might contain - whatever it is, it is bound to be difficult. I remember the regret and worry in Father's voice and cannot help thinking - what if it is worse than merely difficult? That is possible, I argue with myself, but standing in front of the door is not going to get me answers!

As always the room is in semi-darkness. I pull the drapes aside and open a window. Everything looks the way it always did: the skeleton that frightened me when I was small still stands in his corner, yellow-white bony feet sticking out from under his black cover. On Father's desk the rock specimens we gathered together still hold down his to-do notes. And here is the wall of medical literature which belongs to Simon now.

There are hundreds of other books spread out over the other walls, from floor to ceiling. Loosely arranged alphabetically by subjects, and very loosely inside the subject by authors.

I decide to start with "A" for ancient history which would take care of the Egyptians, Chinese, Greeks and Romans. I push the step ladder into the "A" corner, start checking and promptly sneeze into a dust cloud. Obviously Olga has not been at the books for some time. I work myself through dusty volumes until she pulls me away for a cup of tea.

"What you look for?"

"Why pretend you don't know?" I challenge her.

She shrugs. "Not say nothin' now. Say much later," she adds darkly. "Here," she hands me a kitchen apron, "books have dust."

"Yes, I noticed."

Of course she knows. I am angry and relieved at the same time. Angry because Father has kept something from me that he shared with Olga, relieved because she knows and will be someone to talk to, afterwards. Afterwards ...

I feel separate from everybody and everything as I spend a long afternoon searching and checking, except for the few moments when I let myself be side-tracked by the nature books I have always loved. Of course I know

I'm dawdling: I do want to find the notebook, but at the same time I am afraid to. It is so much easier to remember how Father showed me Louis Agassiz's volumes on fish fossils before he told me about his revolutionary theory that Earth had gone through an Ice Age!

It is the same the next day, and the next, and I have already looked through more than half the books. Still nothing. I begin to wonder whether I ought to have asked Father about the size of the notebook - what if it is very small and I have somehow overlooked it? I decide that isn't very likely.

In the afternoon I start on a section devoted to inventions. I used to love to look through a heavy volume about Leonardo da Vinci and his designs for a parachute, a diving bell and other fascinating ideas - but not today. I remind myself of what I am supposed to be doing.

When friends and patients come again to call, Olga pulls me out of the library and gives me a little shove into the living room, reminding me that it is the custom to sit with the visitors. "Is same in Hungary!" she hisses. Well, it may be the custom the world over, but I don't know how to make small talk and I know even less how to cope with the uncomfortable silences that stretch out longer and longer until suddenly everybody begins to speak at the same time.

I am relieved when I can escape because my satchel is at last delivered by the coach driver who, as he puts it, had not expected me to be up and around and in one piece. He says a rock- and mudslide outside Visp halted traffic in both directions for a few days; it has just now been cleared. When he mentions that he is on his way back to Geneva I ask him to wait. Feeling as if a lifetime separated me from my school days I write a quick note to Monique and add that I would still like to come to Paris for a vacation if her parents agree. Meanwhile Olga takes good care of the driver in her kitchen. He leaves, fortified by her good cooking and pleased about the coins I have dropped into his hand. "Don't you worry yourself 'bout that 'brella", he says, carrying the neatly folded coat over his arm, "T'weren't a sturdy one. I'll see the letter gets to your friend quick."

Back to the library the following morning for hours on the English, German and Italian literature shelves.

In the afternoon I go through the larger French section. Without any hope I tackle a six-volume eighteenth-century illustrated collection of French tales of chivalry - all about damsels in distress who have already swooned or are about to do so, decorously of course, while their gallant knights single-handedly perform improbably heroic feats against ogres, fire-belching dragons, gigantic spiders and other beastly perils - on or off their horses. Of course I meant to say steeds: knights would not sit astride common horses! Why would anyone devote six leather-bound books to such nonsense?

They must have been a gift to my father, a very expensive one, too, but the books look like they have never been opened.

I reach for the last volume and have to steady myself on the ladder: from the outside this book looks exactly like the other five volumes, *but it is lighter, much lighter.* Slowly I open it and see that it has been hollowed out, leaving margins on three sides which have been glued together to form a perfect hiding place for Father's notebook! Here it is, resting on top of two pamphlets! I take a quick look at them: 'Cornwall Heraldry' and 'Cornwall Mining'. I don't need to learn about Cornwall now, whatever and wherever that is. The only thing that matters is I have found the notebook. Elated and scared all at the same time I climb down, sit down on the floor and open it.

"For our Aglaia" is written on the first page in his strong, precise hand, precise for a doctor that is. All I have to do is turn the page and start reading. My father was a good man; he would never have done or written about anything that might harm me, I know that, and yet I am afraid. There is no going back once I start reading ...

Olga's annoyed "You deaf, Child? Hundred time I call supper!" makes the decision for me. I am relieved that I can put off reading for a little while.

After we eat I tell her that I am tired and want to go to bed early, something she has tried to get me to do for days.

"About times," she says, "sleep good."

"You, too."

I will have the privacy I need.

Chapter V

"Aglaia, my dearest daughter (this is the way I think of you, our dearest daughter, and I always will) -

I have worried about how to write this for many years. Your mother never wanted you to know. She lived in fear that we might lose you, too, if you knew. After you have read this, you will understand her loving protectiveness, the sadness that came over her at times, and why I could not go against her wishes. After she was taken from us I tried to convince myself that I didn't have to tell you, not yet, but even then I knew that while you have the right to know, I don't have the right to keep this from you. I hope that your kind heart *will help you to understand and to forgive me."*

I had put the notebook down after reading the first sentence.

I had reason to be afraid. "I shall always think of you as our dearest daughter" - why wouldn't he? I *am* his daughter, I *am* their daughter! What has been kept from me, what is there to forgive? I start to read again, from the beginning, and continue.

"Your mother and I were married for almost nine years before our Alicia was born. It had been a difficult pregnancy after two miscarriages, labor was long, and I knew there should not be another child. We rejoiced in our little daughter, but I worried about how small and delicate she remained.

I have a sister? A sister Alicia - and all these years they never told me about her?

Then came the winter of 1846/47, one of the harshest winters our valley ever experienced. Sickness accompanied by high fevers and croup was everywhere; I was kept busy day and night, often traveling far distances from Brig. Sometimes I was not able to return in the evening. Your mother kept everyone but Olga away from Alicia, for fear she might 'catch something'.

My sense of foreboding is growing. Something is going to happen, something bad, I fear ... I am very uneasy, but I have to read on.

"One morning very early, Olga waited for me at the door after one of those absences (I had decided against riding back at night because it had started to snow) and wordlessly pointed upstairs. Your mother was sitting by the window, Alicia who had started to run a fever during the night cradled in her arms. I listened to her chest, noted the restlessness of her little body – and there was nothing I could do. Nothing. Your mother's pleas, "Help her, there must be something you can do!" will always ring in my ears. I tried everything I could think of; at last Alicia fell asleep.

Only minutes later, Benedikt - you remember, the Hallers' oldest son - pounded on our door. He was with his brother and the driver of a party of travelers who had met with an accident, up on the Simplon Road. The carriage had overturned and the driver, unable to get to his passengers, had struggled down the mountain to the Haller farm to try to get help."

I cannot imagine what this accident has to do with me, but - but, if Father writes about it in such detail there must be a reason. More and more unsettled, I continue reading.

Your mother had just finished the tea into which I had put a mild sedative. She was exhausted and it looked like she might give in to sleep. Alicia was asleep in her crib. With all my heart I wanted to stay with them, but thought I might get to the unfortunate travelers in time while there was nothing I could do here. When Olga promised not to budge from your mother's side, I left, telling myself I would be back within the hour.

We trudged up the mountain, Benedikt and Franz pulling the big sled behind them. Why anyone had attempted the Simplon at this time of year was beyond our comprehension, even more so why any driver would agree to take them! Surely someone must have told them that this road is rarely passable between November and April.

Before we could see anything we heard that awful sound, the whinnying of injured horses. Then we spotted the carriage, off the road on its side, half-buried in a huge snowdrift. The horses were still harnessed to it, one must have suffocated in the snow, the other two still thrashed about. I motioned to Benedikt to take a closer look and, if necessary, to use the revolver he had brought along. He fired several shots.

I am wondering, more and more confused - what does this has to do with *me*? Why describe the accident in such detail? Why do I have to know about this, I don't see any connection - but then I can almost hear Father's voice, "Don't be impatient, Aglaia." I go on reading.

"*The carriage door facing us was half open; we succeeded in almost wrenching it off its hinges and I climbed into the opening and peered inside. I could see no signs of life. A gentleman was lying under a trunk which must have fallen on him from the overhead rack; there was no movement, and the angle of his bloodied neck and face could mean only one thing. There must have been a woman in the other corner - all I could see of her was a heap of furs. There was no movement or sound from her either, but we had to make sure. Franz, being the smallest and most agile, lowered himself into the carriage. He called up that the window had shattered (which explained the cuts on the man's face) and that papers were frozen to his hands. I asked Franz to see if the woman might still be alive. "Don't reckon so," he said, after a while, "poor lady's stiff with cold."*

And then - then we all heard that small, plaintive cry and Franz exclaimed, "Holy Mother of God, there must be a babe in here somewhere!" He bent down again, pulled a small fur bundle out from under all the other furs and reached it up to me.

My dearest, dearest Aglaia, there is no other way of telling you this: that was the first time I took you in my arms."

The notebook drops from my hands.

No! No! No! This is not true, this cannot be true, this is wrong, it must be wrong, it is a mistake, a terrible, terrible mistake ... but when he says 'you', he *does* mean me. Me. I understand the words, but not how I can be that infant, that I *am* that infant! I must have misread, misinterpreted something somewhere. I go back to the beginning, even though I know I have not misread, I have not misunderstood. Here it is again, that awful sentence: *That was the first time I took you in my arms.* Eleven words, I count them again, eleven words ... and who I always thought I was, the family that I thought was my family, that I thought belonged to me, my life as I knew it, everything I was linked to - all of this is erased with these eleven words, vanishes.

I pick the notebook up and as my hands touch the leather binding I know that just as this small book is real, so is what I have been reading. I feel ill and crawl into my bed. I want to scream but have no voice. I try to gather my thoughts but there is only fear. I am afraid, so afraid ...

Eventually the sounds of Barry's barking and frantic scratching at my door and Olga's angry voice from downstairs reach through to me. "Take dog out 'fore he break door! Now I say!" Her 'now' is an angry shout. I go out with Barry, ignore the sticks he keeps fetching and rush him back inside.

Back in my room I feel I'll lose my mind, caught in the turmoil of thoughts and pieces of thoughts that whirl around and collide with each other ... I am not who I thought I was ... how could Father say I inherited my interest in science and mathematics from him when he is not my father? That I get my love of reading and pretty things from my mother who is not my mother? ... If only I hadn't found the notebook ... what a silly thought, as if I could ever erase from my memory what Father who is not my father wrote! Who were my parents? Who? And invariably I come back to where and how this nightmare began: why was Father at the old mill when he had his 'accident'? Why?

There are no answers, only so many questions ...

Slowly something else pushes into the jumble of my thoughts: I have not finished reading. I need to know everything else, it cannot be worse than this ...

" ... *That was the first time I took you in my arms. To my great relief I could not detect any injuries on you; all the fur your mother had wrapped around you had prevented the cold from reaching you. A locket which had been placed around your neck had opened; there were no pictures inside. I closed it before I tucked it way down into your clothes. You started to wail loudly, in protest it seemed, and we all cheered! I waited until Benedikt and Franz had pulled the couple from the carriage. I am so very sorry, Aglaia - your parents were beyond help.*

I left the brothers and the driver to the task of bringing them and their belongings down to our hospital and notifying police. I started towards home, holding you to my chest under my coat, anticipating your mother's joy about your addition to our family. Two little girls to raise, two daughters growing up together!

When I reached home, your mother sat where I had left her, only minutes over an hour earlier. Alicia was in her arms. Olga stood next to her, weeping, wringing her hands, shaking her head …

No! … No … I don't want to understand what that tells me, but I know. I knew before I read it: Alicia died, I live. I think I even know what else Father has to tell me …

Olga walked over to me and whispered, "I try 'n try, but she not give little one, not to me … you take, Doctor?"

You started to whimper. I don't know that one can call what I did a conscious or rational decision, it was the only thing I could do: I took Alicia from her mother, I still don't know why she let me, and gave her to Olga; then I put you into her arms and sat down next to her. I don't know whether she heard me, she seemed very far away, but I kept telling her what had happened, that a young couple had perished, that there was no one to give care and

love to their daughter, no one except us. She did not say anything,
but after a while she took the bottle
of warm milk I had asked Olga to
bring up, and still not really with
me, I thought, she fed you. I could
never get her to talk about that
night, not then, not later. Never.
You know that's how she was about
certain things. She kept holding you
for the next few days, as if unable to
let go of you, unwilling even to put
you down into your crib. On the day
I first heard her whispering your
name I dared hope that you had become her daughter, too.

It is important for you to understand
that no one knows about this except
Olga. She swore by all her Saints and
on her mother's grave to keep our secret; I know she will. Kaspar does not
know. Benedikt and Franz were told
that the rescued infant succumbed to
a fever later that night.

You wonder how this is possible.
It was a simple matter to let it be

known that the found child had not
survived, both of you were of about
the same age and had the same col-
or hair and eyes. Not only that, your
mother had kept everybody away
from Alicia for many weeks, fearing
that visitors might bring sickness
into the house. As far as everyone in
Brig knows, the found infant was
laid to rest with her parents.

If you wonder about your name: I
mentioned to Brig's gossipiest woman (you know whom I mean!) that
your mother and I went back and
forth between Alicia and Aglaia
for months but finally settled on
Aglaia. I knew she would be delighted to tell the entire town. She did!

I have had doubts over the years
- doubts which have nothing to
do with you as our daughter. The
doubts are about my right to have
kept the truth from you for so many
years. The more time went by, the
harder it became to tell you. I almost did once, after your mother

*died - but how could I add to your
sadness? Later, I still wanted to
hold on to you, to keep you close.
I'll tell her when she turns twenty or
twenty-one, I told myself, when she
is more mature. There is time, I justified the delay, and meanwhile I'll
write everything down..."*

There are a few more lines, but I cannot read more. All I can think of is how I wish I could make time run backwards, back to when I knew I was Aglaia Andereggen, born and raised in Brig - what do I do with not belonging to the family I knew was mine all my life, about everything unraveling, with all the certainties that anchored my life gone? I want the sameness of my days back. But I have lost Father and with him everything.

I cannot sort out the new questions which swirl around in my head ... I don't even know what my real name is, my parents' names, where they were from, when I was born and where. I know nothing. Not even a simple fact like my birthday.

I need to talk to someone. "Olga!" I tear out of my room. "I know what you meant, the other day. Now I *know!*" I rush to her and she holds me, lets me cry and shout and scream. When I quiet down she leads me into her kitchen, brews two cups of her cure-call herbal tea and makes sure I drink mine while it is hot.

"Now," she says, settling herself on the bench next to me. "I know what happen: you found doctor book, yes? No good be sorry for self. I talk sense for you now."

"Olga!" I start crying again. "I don't feel sorry for myself. I am sad, confused, scared. Why can't you understand that? Olga, Olga, what am I supposed to do?"

"No Olga Olga me!" she says firmly, drying first my tears, then her own. She puts her arms around me. "Think of what important, think only that. Doctor your father all life, no better father in world. No better mother, both love you so much. Only that important!" Her voice rises angrily. "Where be if he not go mountain? He save your life - think only that. Don't you know nothin'?"

"That's right, I don't know anything anymore! Nothing feels right, everything is changed," I sob. "I don't know who I am, not even what my real name is. It's easy for you to say what I have to hold on to, but there is nothing to hold on to - and how is it possible that nobody knows?"

Olga brushes the hair out of my face. "That one easy. Is truth: two little ones, look like, mother say no peoples in house, too much sickness. So: child dies with mother n' father. Peoples knowin' only that!"

This may make sense to others, but it does not help me. "What about my name?" I ask. "What was my name before? I mean I can't imagine ... no other parents would ever have chosen Aglaia. Olga: who named me?"

"Who think? Use brains! Parents!"

"Which parents?"

"True parents!" Olga snaps at me. "Doctor talk Greek ladies, three Graces I think? Mother say to leave Greeks in olden days, she only like one name. Doctor ask, "Which one, dear?" She tell, doctor he say he already know, so you baptized Aglaia. And cry loud, much louder than pastor words! His words, they all drown!" She smiles at the memory and hugs me. "Not remember other two names."

I do remember, though, and suppose I ought to be grateful. Aglaia is unusual but a sight better than Thalia or, heaven forbid, Euphrosyne. When I used to complain about my name Father used to tease me, what if he could have talked Mother into Agnodice after a fourth century B.C. Athenian woman doctor? "Mother would never have agreed to that!" I had always come back at him ...

But what does a name matter when I have lost who I am - how can I make Olga understand that? "I don't know who I am anymore, why don't you understand that?"

She shrugs. "Why problem? Yesterday, today, tomorrow - you same girl all days. Nice girl when not in bad moods, when not run to troubles."

"That's not what I man," I protest. "Why don't you understand? I cannot be the same girl, not with everything changed. I need ... I don't know what I need ... find something, but what? ... I don't know what, I just don't know ... or maybe I do know? ... I think ... no, I know ... I have to find out who my other parents were, try to find out. Can't you at least understand that much?"

"Already know that," Olga sighs. "Knowin' long, long time. But not rush, Child. Think, think hard."

Something else has just occurred to me. "Didn't anybody ever come looking for my parents, the other couple, even the driver?"

"Not knowin'. I cook now. Food not happen from nothin'. Take dog out." She gives me a quick hug. "Not be out sorts, Child, no good."

"What's so good about being '*in* sorts', if there is such a thing?" I answer nastily and immediately know that Father would have raised his eyebrows at what he used to call my 'prickly defensiveness' before he'd make me apologize. I also know that now she will attack her kitchen chores as if the Furies were after her; it is what she does when she is upset or angry. If only I could lose myself so completely in something, anything ...

I take care of Barry, go back upstairs and pick up Father's notebook again. There are only a dozen more lines. I notice that his handwriting has changed a little; it is smaller, less assured. Written at a later date, I guess ...

Sending you to school in Geneva was

a difficult decision; you will understand why I insisted on it when you see the contents of the small trunk which is everything that could be salvaged from their carriage. Your parents must have sent luggage ahead to where they were going; they traveled with very little.

I know that a difficult time is ahead for you and wish it didn't have to be so, but please remember that you have been our dearest daughter for (almost) all of your life. Nothing can change that. You **are** my dearest daughter. I expect and understand that you want to find out if you have another family somewhere. You have my blessing for this search, but don't do it alone. Ask your Uncle Kaspar for help,

Your Father."

Chapter VI

I suppose logic would dictate, 'Go up to the attic and find that trunk!' but there is no room for logic in my head. How and where do I look for answers for questions I don't even know how to ask? Only one question always rears up out of the confusion: why did Father ride up to the old mill late at night instead of coming home?

I decide to go for a walk - not that I expect the air to clear my mind or that walking could outpace grief. But perhaps it will tire me out enough so that I can stop thinking ....

Of course Barry squeezes by me as soon as I open the door.

He charges ahead of me. Without a conscious thought I start up towards the cemetery. I had avoided it after Mother died, except on her birthday when Father insisted we put flowers on her grave. I wonder - when is my other mother's birthday? When is *my* birthday? I don't even know when I was born, and where. Thoughts skitter around in my head, aimlessly, disappear before I can follow them.

I open the iron gates, leaving a disconsolate Barry, tail thumping pleadingly, on the grass outside. For a moment I stand at Father's grave. The earth hasn't settled yet and the flowery tributes, piled high one on top of another, have reached varying stages of decay. Despite the afternoon sun I feel chilled. But then the unfamiliar sense of a new loyalty pushes me towards the older graves. I have no names to help me find them, only a date.

At last I find them, in the small fenced-in 'foreigners' corner' where mountain climbers who have met with accidents and other unclaimed bodies are laid to rest. Two plain stone markers, they have only the initials W.J.T. and T.T. chiseled into the stone and the date 1847. The smaller maker in front of them bears only the same date. My parents and Alicia ...

I wonder ... did my mother come here, where her Alicia is buried? She must have, perhaps while I was in school? How hard it must have been for her, living with this secret every day of her life. I had never thought of this before.

I stand there for a long time until Barry's insistent bark reminds me that it is time to go back.

Olga and Simon had not waited supper for me but are still sitting at the table. "You gone long times," Olga scolds, "I worry, Child."

"I had to be by myself."

Simon looks up from his plate. "What's the matter? Don't you feel well?"

How could I be feeling well? "No." I hadn't meant to sound so curt.

"What is wrong?" he asks again.

I shrug. "I have a headache."

"You might feel better after you eat something."

As if food could help ... but I realize I that am hungry.

"I've been waiting to talk to you. I hope you don't mind that your father left me the surgery and his medical books, and gave me the opportunity to live here. It was extremely generous of him." He begins the process of lighting his pipe.

"Yes, he was a very generous man, but why would I mind? I don't need medical books; it's not like I'll ever study to be a doctor. I am glad you have them."

"Well, then I'm glad that you are glad."

"Didn't you think I would be?" I challenge him, more sharply than I intended.

Simon who is still concentrating on his pipe looks up. "I miss him, too, very much."

But I miss *my father*. To Simon he was only a mentor,

the man he worked with - how can he compare his loss to mine? If there is sorrow in his voice I don't want to hear it.

"I have my work," he continues; "work does not change what happened, what is, but it helps one get through the day. What about you? Wouldn't it help if you had something to occupy your time? Any ideas, plans?"

I answer, "I don't know yet," and realize that isn't quite true. The same thought has been going around in my head, vague, unformed. It all depends on whether the trunk in the attic will give me some answers.

"I have been thinking I might go away for a while," I announce, surprising myself.

"W-w-what say? You not like school!" Olga sputters and almost drops the platter she is drying. Simon manages to tighten the grip on his pipe just in time.

"Well, why shouldn't she?" He sounds annoyingly reasonable. "Doctor thought she might want to do some traveling."

"When he say this?"

"Could both of you please not talk about me as if I wasn't sitting right in front of you?" I interrupt them. "I'm not going back to that school. If you must know, I thought I might go to Paris to be with Monique for a while – we've talked about this for a long time. I might go elsewhere afterwards, perhaps ..."

Olga recovers sufficiently from her shock to ask, "Paris? Paris in France?"

"That Paris, yes."

Olga crosses herself and lets me know that she holds a very low opinion of all things French, French morals in particular. "France," she says darkly, giving the word an intonation of intense distrust, "You know what happen buta lányok there?" Before she can recite a list of misfortunes that might befall 'silly girls' - among which she likes to include me - I go over to her and hug her. "Don't worry, I'm not leaving tomorrow!"

She pulls out of my grasp and mutters, "I not make joke!" before she attacks pots and pans with unnecessary vigor.

"Let me know if I can help you in any way," Simon says, again in that new irritating and flat voice. He rises from the table and leaves. I wish he'd stay, but he isn't the same Simon. Let him go, I tell myself, this is only one more thing that has changed in my life. Along with everything else.

The attic. Go, I tell myself, go. Go. I am tired but not sleepy and grab a lantern.

I had forgotten about the old boards and I jump when they creak; I have not been up here in years. Holding the light high I play its beam over the clutter accumulated over many years - boxes, luggage, broken furniture, crockery, tools, climbing gear and ropes, lamp shades, blankets, an antlered hat stand and the clock that has most of its insides missing, zithers and three large trunks, unlocked, empty ...

At last I find the small trunk, covered by an old table-cloth and wedged into a dark corner at the other end of the attic. I brush off the cobwebs and decide to carry it down to my room where the light is better.

Eager and hesitant at the same, I try Father's key. It feels a little stiff at first but suddenly catches. The latch springs open and the first thing I see is a beautiful lac-quered jewelry box lying on top of silky blue fabric - a lady's shawl perhaps? It see that it covers yellowed pa-pers and a baby's christening gown.

Papers first. They might tell me names, places ... they don't. All they give me are the same initials, W.J.T. - on notes and drawings of trees, shrubs, herbs, flowers and at what altitudes they have been found. And a notation to compare salt and copper mining. Why, I wonder? The pages are smudged, probably from snow, and I can imagine what the brown spots are ... written by a man, I decide, but nothing tells me why. No name, no place, no destination ... 'W' for Werner? Wilhelm?

Next I take a look at the christening gown. It is made of embroidered lace and looks very expensive. No markings on it either, but I feel very sure of this as I recover it with the blue shawl - love and care must have gone into its selection. Who bought it? My mother? My grandmother? Why were my parents traveling with it, isn't that something one leaves at home? Well, perhaps not. There are other infant clothes and a small blanket. Where was home? There is so much I may never know.

I look at the jewelry box again. Intricate mother-of-pearl decorations cover the lid. Looking more closely, I discover that several T's are cleverly hidden among the stylized leaves and flowers. 'T' for what? Therese? Tatiana? A Russian name? Not very likely, but no other 'T' names come to mind.

I don't know what I expect when I open the box, certainly not the two miniatures. One is of a dark-haired, pretty young woman, but the other one - it is like looking at my own face! There is no mistaking the resemblance. I have inherited my mother's hazel eyes while my father's are blue, but the high forehead and curly blonde hair, the long straight nose, wide mouth - and that dimple? I have it, too! He looks fair-skinned, as I am. I wonder whether he, too, used to get a sprinkling of freckles in summer ...

Sudden sadness chokes me. My parents are not blank faces anymore, the paintings have made them real - they look so young. For the first time I think of their last day, their fate of dying in the dark and the cold, my father lying under that trunk, unable to get to his wife and child; my mother trying to keep me warm, even as she feels the cold encroaching ... I may never learn anything about them unless I can discover their names. But I have nothing to go on, nothing.

I crawl into bed and punch and thump at my pillow, but cannot pound it into a comfortable shape. How do I look for two people when all I know of them are their initials? I have not only lost Father, I have lost everybody, everything. Everything ... I give in to the tears which keep coming and don't stop ...

When I wake up, still in yesterday's rumpled clothes, and see my red swollen eyes staring back at me in the mirror, I promise myself not to cry myself to sleep again. Or at least I shall *try* not to: I cannot face the prospect of well-meaning people noticing and trying to comfort me. *They* may feel better for it, but I don't, having to listen to them. I remember how Father used to say that giving in to self-pity makes everything more difficult, but this is not self-pity. It is a sadness so deep that there are no words for it.

I open the jewelry box which still lies next to my pillow and I realize that I never looked what else might be inside. I lift out the velvet-lined tray which had held the miniatures and, nestled under a double strand of pearls see a man's ring. Large and heavy - solid gold? When I turn it over I immediately know that I am holding something important: with its three rows of three small gold rounds on black, the ring is an exact match to my locket!

I try to remember what Father had said when he gave me the locket on my twelfth birthday - not very much except, of course, to take very good care of it and to wear it only on Sundays for the time being. When I wanted to know where he had bought it and if there was a special meaning to the gold rounds, he only said that it was supposed to be quite old and that he'd had it for a long time - but now I know that he did not buy it! I had asked him again what those gold rounds meant and he repeated that he didn't know, adding, "Who knows? Perhaps you will learn their meaning, some time." I had forgotten about that, too, but what is important is this: my locket has ceased to be merely a pretty piece of jewelry. I have a ring that matches it. Both must belong to a family. My family ...

Suddenly something reminds me: the botanical notes are in *English* - how could I have let the significance of that escape me? My father must have been English: not Werner or Wilhelm, I think - perhaps William? And suddenly Father's insistence that I be fluent in that language ceases to be a whim.

But where do I go from here, where do I look for answers? Where?

Simply by asking myself 'where?' I know. When I used to go to Father with questions he'd say, "The simplest thing would be for me to give you the answer if I know it, but you'll remember it much longer if you look it up yourself - so off you go!" There may be something in the Cornwall Heraldry Book. Father put those two pamphlets with the notebook for a reason, didn't he? What is Cornwall? The name of a place?

Well, I find out that Cornwall is indeed a place, part of England, a peninsula in the Southwest with its westernmost terrain named, very aptly, Land's End. I do not bother with the names of towns and villages (many seem to have unpronounceable names) and skip ahead to Cornwall's early history, one part of which is very interesting indeed:

In the 9th century, after one of the crusades, fifteen bezants (i.e. Byzantine gold coins) were paid by the people of Cornwall to the Saracens in ransom for the release of their Earl of Cornwall. Four hundred years later one of his descendants built himself a castle near Tintagel and chose those fifteen bezants on a black background as his coat of arms, adding a black eagle on top and a lion rampant at the bottom.

I take out the ring and look at it again. Both locket and ring have three rows of three bezants, not fifteen, and neither eagle nor lion. Well, both being considerably smaller than shields, they could not hope to accommodate fifteen bezants *and* two animals. Before I know it I am off on a daydream in which I am one of the Earl's long-lost descendants - it lasts seconds only before common sense drops me down to earth again! How silly! A postscript cautions readers (I suppose especially impressionable ones like me!) that the ransom story may be more legend than fact. It doesn't matter: gold bezants point to Cornwall!

Since I have only the dimmest notion of who the Saracens were and none at all of what makes a lion rampant, I think I had better pursue that, too. Father, no doubt, would say, "Don't be lazy, Aglaia, go ask the brothers," meaning Jakob and Wilhelm Grimm of fairy tale fame. Tired of the daily worries about where their next meal would come from while they collected and published their fairy tales, they decided to compile a German dictionary. That venture was so successful that they were able to concentrate on their fairy tales *and* eat hearty meals every day from then on. Father purchased all the dictionary volumes as they became available.

Back to the library, where I find both answers. Saracens are what Europeans called all Arabs and Muslims in the Middle Ages, well into later centuries.

I also find the 'lion rampant'. The brothers explain him as a lion facing left with both forepaws raised and standing on one leg. They don't explain why one cannot say 'rampant lion' which seems less awkward than 'lion rampant' ...

Cornwall - I put everything except the ring back into the jewelry box and into the trunk and wonder how one gets from Brig to Cornwall. In vain I try to conjure up a dimly remembered map - to Geneva first, then north into France, across the Channel and to London, I suppose. And from there - more coaches? How many miles, how many days of travel? What would it cost? Do I have enough money? What if I don't?

I decide to slip the ring onto my locket chain, keeping both hidden under my clothes, and for the first time ever I see merit in those ruffled blouses.

Then I turn to the Mining Glossary. Wheals, whim ropes, kibbles winzes, slag, proceeding to grass - they all sound like a foreign language. I don't need to know this yet; there will be time enough to read about this later, if and when the connection to Cornwall is established. Not if, *when*! I set the small volume aside for the time being.

I may have to go to England which means travel expenses, and that may be a problem, a large one. I'll have to speak to Uncle Kaspar ... and give him the notebook for safe-keeping! I am jolted by the realization that the notebook is the only proof of what happened so many years ago; it needs to be kept in a very safe place! I am relieved that, at least sometimes, I am able to think clearly again.

Still feeling dazed, I go downstairs for breakfast. I feel - not better, I am still very far away from that, but not as hopeless and helpless as in all the days since I was summoned into Madame's presence.

Simon has finished his meal and looks at me. "You should try to spend more time outdoors, Aglaia," he says, "you look a little peaked. Olga tells me that you spend hours every day in the library. Why this sudden interest in books, may I ask?"

"No, you may not! Besides, what do you mean by 'sudden'? I have always loved books and reading." The old Simon would have remembered that. I tell the new one that there is nothing sudden about my interest in books and that I can do without his sarcastic comments about my looks. He withdraws into hurt silence and leaves. Immediately I am sorry - why can't we talk to each other anymore?

"Why do you tell him everything I do?" I lash out at Olga.

"Is secret that? I not know!" Olga doesn't take sass from anybody. "Why so angry, Child?"

"To start with - don't you think I am too old to be called Child? And I think I have plenty to be angry about!"

"Many ways lookin' to ... to ... er ... " She cannot find the right word and throws out 'valsami'. Before I can remind her that I have not become fluent in Hungarian overnight she explains that valsami means 'something'. "So: sad, yes. Confuse, also yes. But angry? No!"

"Well, you know what I mean!" I am not in the mood for quibbling over words. "Haven't you noticed how impossible Simon has been, ever since I've come home? If he doesn't tell me what to do he sulks or is so damnably stiff ... sorry, Olga, I know you don't like me to use any of the Devil's wicked words ... what *is* the matter with him?"

"You not know, you not see?" A sly smile creeps over her face. "Mind a ketten."

"Olga, p-l-e-a-s-e stop speaking Hungarian to me! What is 'mind a ketten'? Why on earth should I watch a chain?"

"What say?" She frowns. "No say chain. Say *two no see!*" She holds up two fingers.

Two no see? I have to think about that for a moment before I understand. "Wait, you mean we two - we don't see?"

"Yes, yes, but more. More."

"More what?"

Olga puts both hands over her eyes.

"You mean we don't see? We don't see at all? ... You don't mean that we are both blind, or do you?"

She smiles and nods emphatically.

"I think that is a stupid thing to say and nothing to smile about. The sooner I leave the better. The two of you are welcome to each other." Not waiting to see the hurt that I know will be on her face, I storm out of the kitchen and up to my room. I throw myself on my bed and stare at the ceiling which still needs painting.

I am already sorry. I should not let myself get at odds with Olga. I know she means well, especially when she is inconveniently outspoken. It is her way. Why do I expect her to understand? No one does, no one can. I don't know what bothers Simon - and what am I supposed to do with his polite aloofness? He has not hinted, not with one single word, that he will miss me - not that it would make me change my plans, but I would have liked to hear him say, "I'll miss you Aglaia ... ."

Home doesn't feel like home any more - how could it, it is not home. Angrily, I wipe at the tears I seem unable to control. I do nothing all day, and the nights are worse. That's when I cannot turn off my thoughts; night thoughts are sadder and more frightening than the ones that cling to me like shadows during the day. I don't sleep well, and when I wake up I linger in bed. I have never done that before, but I don't know what to do about those first moments when there is that small flicker of a hope that it was only a bad dream - when I have to understand all over again what has happened. Why get out of bed? Why get dressed? Eventually I rouse myself, only to spend the days in a fog of doing nothing. Olga lets me go through a few days in this manner, limiting herself to disapproving tongue-clucking, much head-shaking and dark Hungarian mutterings.

But then, one morning early, she marches into my room, pulls me out of bed and sits down next to me. "Elég, elég, Child! Elég!"

I know that means 'enough, enough!' She lectures me, several times over, because I don't understand what she means at first - that I am not honoring my father's memory being such a 'henyélö', that he saved my life and that I had better start doing something with what he has given me. She ends with, "And I means *now! Not morrow!*"

"I think I understand," I finally say, grudgingly, "but what is henye...?"

"Henyélö?" It takes her several attempts at explaining until we agree that it must be Hungarian for lazybones. I don't bother to argue that lazy has nothing to do with it because I am glad she has jolted me out of my lethargy. I don't have to tell her; she already knows.

If I am serious about leaving, and I am, I need to see Uncle Kaspar. The church bells have just finished tolling. Ten o'clock - as good a time as any to call on him, do a great deal of explaining and see about travel funds. Dimly I remember something about not having any financial worries but still think I must have misheard.

We chat pleasantly for a few minutes; then he enquires about the purpose of my visit. I tell him that, among other concerns, I need to talk to him about money.

"Of course," he nods, "I have expected that. May I suggest that, for the time being, you receive the same monthly allowance your father, may he rest in peace, had ..."

"That is not exactly what I have in mind," I interrupt him. "I need, what I meant to say is, I would like to have a sum large enough to pay for travel to France, possibly also to England, perhaps to remain there for some time." There, I have said it all in one breath, the way I rehearsed it on the way over, but I don't know how to tell him the rest.

You can never tell whether Uncle Kaspar is taken by surprise or not. "England?" he repeats mildly, "I assume you have a compelling reason for wanting to travel there?"

I put the notebook on his desk, keeping my hand on it. "Well, I have always wanted to go, my best friend lives in Paris and has invited me, and I just need to go away for a while."

He nods, then looks straight at me and asks, "I understand your need to go away for a while, Aglaia, but there is more to it, isn't there?"

"Yes, there is." How do I begin telling him?

He waits. Then, perhaps sensing my unease, he says, "First let me tell you again that as your father's oldest friend and lawyer I intend to look out for you, not only to manage your affairs. Secondly, anything that passes between us will be held in the strictest confidence. It will never leave this room. Thirdly: I cannot in all good conscience let you travel abroad without knowing why and where, without knowing how to remain in touch with you."

Father had thought the world of him. He had called him good-hearted and God-fearing, straight as an arrow if somewhat stiff-necked and set in his ways, thoughtful and trustworthy and honest as the day is long, the most intelligent and well-read man he had ever met who was also 'blessed' with a great affection for details - and all this in a man on the safe side of sixty! I had never asked but assume the expression means below sixty rather than above. If I want his help, and I do, I have to answer him honestly. I slide the notebook towards him. "After you read this, please keep it in a safe place for me."

He reads in silence, every now and then shaking his head, then sits for a while and thinks. When he looks up he says, "This is your father's handwriting, I know it well, and it is an incredible account, I hardly know what to say. I had no idea. And I cannot imagine how confusing and difficult this is for you to try to understand, to come to terms with." I quickly wipe my eyes while he rereads the last page; lately kind words always bring on tears.

"Now do you understand?"

He nods. "Your father mentions two booklets?"

I explain what they are about and why I think that Cornwall is a good place to start.

"Cornwall ... yes, of course. A rather remote British area, I believe. Is that all the proof you have?"

"No, I have miniatures of my parents. And this." I show him the paintings and the ring and remind him that the ring matches my locket. That puts him at a loss for words again. He looks at me and then back at my father's miniature; I know he has noticed the resemblance. After a long pause he assures me again that my secret is safe with him, that he will help me in any way he can, but that under no circumstances am I to attempt to do anything on my own. He also asks who would travel with me.

I am prepared for the question and tell him that my friend Monique Chevalier's brother is supposed to travel from Paris to London on business, that all we have to do is agree on a mutually convenient date.

"That looks to be a satisfactory arrangement where France and a Channel crossing are concerned. What about England?"

"I don't know. I was hoping ... perhaps you know of someone ...?"

"I certainly do." He reaches for stationery, addresses an envelope, writes a short letter, and slides both over to me. "Hold on to this. It will introduce you to an old friend and colleague of mine, Sir Arthur Harrington. He is a London barrister". Lawyer, he adds in case I am not familiar with the term, which I am not. "The correct way to address him, by the way, is either by his full name or as Sir Arthur, not as Sir Harrington. I shall write to him to expect you; I know he will assist you in every way possible – as a matter of fact, always write to me at his address; your letters will reach me more quickly. And remember: urgent messages can be sent by telegraph now." He leans back in his chair. "What a marvelous invention that is. Are you aware that in 1858, only a few years ago, Queen Victoria exchanged telegraph greetings with the American President, Buchanan I think his name was. Over such a distance, amazing, isn't it?"

I nod although I am not able to summon any enthusiasm for queenly/presidential conversations at the moment. I start to thank him, but he holds up his hand.

"No thanks are necessary, but please wait several weeks so all arrangements can be completed. And to get back to your question concerning money: I shall have funds transferred to the Bank of London. I am sure Sir Arthur or one of his clerks will assist you with withdrawals and everything else ... wait, I just thought of something." He reaches into the depths of a desk drawer, pulls out paper money and coins and separates them into three neat piles. "It is always a good idea to familiarize yourself with other currencies: here are some new Swiss francs for the first leg of your journey; French coins and lastly English money. English money is quite different from ours: there are twelve pennies (or pence) to a shilling and twenty shillings to a pound. I think the term guinea is still used for 21 shillings, but guinea coins may no longer be in circulation. That's it for money matters - however I would like to suggest that I take your ring and the portraits for safekeeping, too."

I had given that a great deal of thought and tell him that I want to keep them with me; what other proof of who I am do I have? I assure him that I will be very careful before he has a chance to remind me. "There is one more thing, Uncle Kaspar," I add, "will you see to it that Olga and Simon ... when I am away ..." My voice breaks.

"Of course I shall keep an eye on them," he said kindly and pulls out his pocket watch. "Write to me often. I cannot impress on you strongly enough: *do not undertake anything without Sir Arthur's counsel.* Naturally I want to see you before you leave; I may have more information and additional pounds for you then." He checks the watch again. "Is there anything else?"

I shake my head 'no'. I know I have already taken up much of his time. I thank him, plant a quick kiss on his dry wrinkled cheek and leave. He has thought of everything. He always does.

This has gone pretty well, I think. Now talking to Simon, that will be an entirely different matter, but I do owe him an explanation. When he disappears into the library after supper, again wordlessly, I follow him.

"Can I speak to you for a minute?"

He looks up from his book and puts down his pen. "Certainly. Sit down, please."

He never used to be so stiff, so formal. I tell him

about my meeting with Uncle Kaspar, and that I would be leaving within a few weeks' time and why. He looks stunned when I tell him about the contents of Father's notebook and has trouble believing my story until I show him the ring and the miniatures.

"Of course you must try to find your family," he says, showing no trace of emotion. "You do resemble your father; there might be a family somewhere who doesn't even know you exist." Naturally your secret is safe with me." He stands up, wishes me a safe journey and success in my search, *and then he shakes my hand and leaves the room!* As if I were an acquaintance whom he will not see again the next day, when I have just told him I would not be leaving for about a *month*! On his way out he promises to make sure Barry gets plenty of exercise before I can ask him, then the door closes and he is gone.

Why? I am not leaving tomorrow! Where does his sudden, limitless capacity for irritating me come from? And another thing, usually meticulous about putting the books he has consulted back on their shelves, he has left all of them open on the desk and the ink pot uncovered before he left ... that is so not like him!

Why do I bother wondering? Why do I keep looking for something that is not there? Angry and sad at the same time I cap the ink but leave the books. The only thing I can count on him for is taking Barry for long walks.

I can hardly bear to think about him - Barry, not Simon! I used to miss him very much during the school year, and now I am going so much farther away, and I don't know for how long ...

A few days later I sit down with Olga.

"*Now* you say what happen?" she says gruffly, pleating and re-pleating the edge of her apron the way she does when something worries her.

I explain why I haven't said anything earlier: that first I had to do a lot of thinking, then I had to see Uncle Kaspar, and that I also had to wait for a reply from Monique's brother, but now I am ready. When she realizes that I will leave, most likely within a month, she cries. Despite all assurances and protestations she keeps sobbing - because of the terrible things that could befall a young girl in a godless large city, she repeats. I know it is really because she loves me and will miss me.

Finally I plead, "Olga, please, please no more terrible things and no more tears," and give her my handkerchief. She dries her eyes and, still sniffling, tucks it into her pocket.

"Put back after wash - oh, sorry, I forget." She fishes around in her apron pocket and pulls out a letter from Monique that had been delivered while I was out.

I go up to my room to read it. This is what Monique writes:

"My dearest, dearest Aglaia,

First let me tell you how sad I am for you and with you. I cannot imagine how hard it is to lose a father, especially through an accident for which there is no explanation. I shall always remember how nice he was to me the few times we met. I envied you just a little bit because the two of you were so close and you talked to each other so freely about so many things. I love Papa dearly, but his mind is always on business, even when he talks to me ...

I am glad that Linette helped you get away. She misses you and is worried about losing her position, but I am going to tell Maman that I would like her to travel home with me. I may know more about that later.

You must be curious to hear the latest school news: I wish you could have witnessed the confusion your sudden departure put Madame into First there was the most awful row between Madame and our 'favorite' teacher. Madame's voice, raised to most unladylike screeches, could be heard throughout the entire school! And when they found out that you had left, you should have heard Mr. Thornton curse, so loud, such vulgar language! Absolutely shocking ...

Next thing we hear Madame screaming: it seems her precious cat had knocked over one of her precious cups which shattered. He lapped up the spilled chocolate and then he vomited all over her precious carpet. And an hour later the poor cat was dead! Can you believe it? At first I thought that probably he was not only very fat but also very old; I asked around and found out that he was only 5, maybe 6. My grandmother's cat is still around and is either 14 or 15, depending on who (whom?) you ask. Well, you know more about animals, living in the country the way you do. Can you find out if cats, fat or not, can die from too much chocolate?

The other mystery is that our Mr. T. disappeared the same day. Nobody knows why and where to; we were only told that he was not expected back. Madame took to her bed and has stayed there ever since with "la grande migraine". Most of the girls have gone home already, including me, with Linette (Maman said yes).

Please write and tell me about your plans. Jean-Philippe says don't forget to let him know when *you'll be arriving in Paris. I am so happy that we will be together soon!*

Forever your best friend
Monique

I fold the letter and put it away. Chocolate may not be good for animals in general, I don't know a thing about that, and it is always sad when a pet dies, but I cannot worry about Madame's or anybody else's cat. Not now. Not when every day I think about Father's accident, his notebook and how it has changed my life ...

As agreed, I see Uncle Kaspar again and show him Monique's letter which confirms that I will not be leaving Paris unaccompanied. His eyebrows rise when the reads the first part of the letter and he mutters, "Strange, very strange indeed," but then he hands me 'Charles Dickens' account of riding in a London Omnibus' which he copied from a London newspaper sent to him some years earlier by his lawyer friend. "This will give you an idea of what to expect, getting around in a big city," he says. "It was published several years ago, but I doubt conditions are greatly changed. For what it is worth, the London General Omnibus Company is still supposed to the best one; fares probably are still sixpence."

I am touched by his solicitude and decide to go to the booking office on my way home.

At first I think that I am the only customer, but suddenly I become aware of someone standing so uncomfortably close behind me that I feel his breath on my neck. I half-turn and in my frostiest voice say, "You are standing too close, Monsieur!" to the young man who seems inordinately interested in my conversation with the ticket clerk; he even has the effrontery to ask where I am going! With Uncle Kaspar's "always be on your guard" fresh in my ears I put on a haughty look before I turn my back to him. As soon as my reservation is completed, I hurry home. I look back a few times but do not see him again.

I pack and repack several times, remembering Linette's efficiency. Well, I am not going to have a Linette with me from now on, so I had better learn to take care of things myself. I spend my days doing almost nothing except worrying about Father's notebook and the future until the day of my departure arrives.

Simon, more detached and therefore more irritating than ever, wishes me a safe journey, again the night before.

I am not surprised but amazed how hurtful correctness can be.

When I complain about his aloof manner, that new infuriating detachment of his, and wonder again what causes it, Olga rolls her eyes. "Already say what think.

Not say again." Word for word she repeats the advice she had given me every day, ever since I announced that I was leaving. Not wanting to spoil our last moments together, I nod to everything, especially to being careful. She crushes me in an embrace that says more than words.

The last night at home I feel more restless than ever. I keep waking up and listening to the silence around me, sleep for a short while, only to listen to the silence again. Everything that has happened crowds into my mind, together with new questions about what may yet be ... this may be the last time I sleep in my bed, my room, my house, for a long time, perhaps forever. My house ... which doesn't feel like my home anymore.

Saying good-bye will be difficult ...

Chapter VII

Saying good-bye is easier than I expected because after that polite and emotionless 'bon voyage' of the night before, Simon has again left very early in the morning. I promise Olga again that I could not tell her *when* it would be, but that I *would* come back. This morning she wears her stoic face when we hug god-bye and I am the one in need of a handkerchief.

After spending the night in Geneva, I am looking forward to the novelty of the first travel day after Geneva, but it is dull and uncomfortable. The day is hot and humid, and it is difficult to get used to the bad odors that live in our large coach which is also old and worn. The stained brown curtains have seen better days and the closed windows rattle loudly - they have to remain closed in order to keep the large swarms of horseflies out which seem intent on traveling with us. The coach sways and jolts a great deal, especially when the driver sends it careening full tilt towards a coaching inn while the man sitting next to him blows ear-shattering blasts on his horn in order to announce our arrival - as if anyone with two ears could be unaware of it! On the other hand I do admire the speed with which horses are exchanged.

I have taken Monique's letter with me and reread it for the third time. The argument between Madame and Mr. Thornton doesn't matter to me at all, but when I think back to that morning what begins to strike me as odd is that Madame changed her mind so suddenly. What was it she could not do? Why did she let me leave when minutes earlier she had been so adamant that I stay and drink that hot chocolate with them. And then she wept. Nothing about this makes sense ...

The second day is anything but dull.

To begin with, our new vehicle is smaller and clean-er, if perhaps too liberally scented by an elderly lady's perfume, even with our windows dropped down some. According to signposts we are on our way to Nevers and have just entered a forest of oaks, white birches and firs. Our new driver, a Frenchman, has switched from sing-ing loudly and off-key to cursing the sorry state of all French roads. Suddenly, other sounds mix in with his voice and the coach comes to an abrupt halt. Both doors are yanked open and two sinister-looking characters, one on each side, faces hidden behind dark kerchiefs, mo-tion with big, ugly pistols for everybody to get down. No, this cannot be happening! I am about to comply - what else can one do against pistols? - when the elderly lady who sits across from me collapses in a faint. No, only a near-faint: her eyelids keep fluttering. Her maid, paralyzed with fright, tries to scream, but her mouth opens and closes without making a sound.

"Vite, vite! Out with you, hurry!"

No, this cannot be happening! A hold-up will ruin my plans! Are those two men merely waving their pistols around, or do they really mean to shoot us if we don't follow orders? Unfortunately they look very threatening and I remind myself: whatever happens, I mustn't attract attention to the fact that I'm wearing jewelry inside my blouse! One bandit, seeing that the two women are not moving at all, pulls himself up into the coach and slaps first the maid's face, hard, and then her mistress. He jumps back down and hollers, "Out, out! Vite, vite! I said hurry!"

I was brought up to respect my elders and I hate violence. More than that, I cannot let those two crooks ruin everything! Noticing that the gentleman who has been dozing next to me is stirring at last and stealthily working a pistol out from under his coat I draw myself up and take two steps, as if getting ready to step down - but instead I grab the lady's walking stick which leans in the corner. It feels sturdy enough. Good. Before I know what I am doing, I lean down and the cane in my hand strikes the bandit's pistol arm with considerable force. He drops his weapon, clutches his arm and yells, "Bloody 'ell, she broke me arm!" I manage to hit him once more, this time on his other shoulder. Then I jump down and kick his weapon out of the way. And *then* - well, that is when my knees buckle into wobbly jelly and I have to lean against the dusty coach or I would have wound up sitting in the dirt! I sense that locket and ring are where they are supposed to be, thank God, and then it dawns on me - what a splendid example of acting before thinking that was, not to mention violent!

Luckily our driver has overpowered the other bandit, and the gentleman with the pistol keeps it trained on the one who has pulled off his kerchief and, supporting his arm, moans loudly, "Bloody 'ell, she broke me arm, I swear she did, bloody 'ell!"

"On the ground, both of you!" he threatens them. "Shut up, both of you. Not another word!"

Then he turns towards me. "Allow me to introduce myself, Mademoiselle: Geoffrey Harwood, at your service. I must say, I do admire your courage!" He has a nice smile.

Courage? Father would have done a lot more than shake his head at this. Olga, in a stream of exasperated Hungarian, would have called it the greatest foolhardy stupidity she'd ever witnessed. I myself can hardly believe what I did. I watch as the bandits' hands are securely tied behind their backs. "What happens now?" I ask.

"What usually happens," the driver answers with a shrug, "after we tie 'em up we dump 'em, pardon me we leave 'em at the nearest préfecture. That would be Nevers. That means a delay for us and," he points to Mr. Harwood, "Monsieur will have to remain as witness." He shrugs again. "It happens, Mademoiselle, what can one do?"

Obviously Mr. Harwood has no intention of being a witness anywhere because he immediately says, "Out of the question!" I have meetings and appointments in London which cannot be postponed ... after all, nothing of consequence happened, no one was injured" – he leans into the coach, smiles at the lady and corrects himself - "I beg your pardon, Madame, *seriously* injured; they didn't get their hands on our valuables." He looks at her, then at me, obviously expecting us to agree.

Well, I too need to get to Paris without delay or Jean-Philippe might have to leave without me. I, too, cannot afford to waste time waiting around for a court hearing.

"I really must insist that we proceed," Mister Harwood repeats. "I am sure Madame is anxious to be back within the comforts of her lovely home as soon as possible, isn't that so?" He steps up into the coach, smiles down at her, takes her hand and pats it reassuringly. It seems to me that he is wasting a lot of charm on an old woman, but if that is what it takes to get her to agree ....

"Oh, if only I was there already!" she interrupts her moans to send a coquettish smile up to him (She must be seventy and I do not exaggerate, she does!). He extricates his hand and turns to me. I nod my assent.

After a quick conversation with the driver, Mr. Harwood walks over to the bandits and talks to them - threateningly, from what I can see. He must have ordered them to disappear if they knew what was good for them: hands still tied, they have some difficulty getting to their feet before they take off into the forest like a pair of frightened rabbits.

After this he turns to be an attentive and amusing travel companion, although I do wonder why he slipped the driver money. I am definitely encountering much that I do not know or understand. Since he keeps stumbling over Andereggen I permit him to address me by my first name. Why not, it is for a few hours only.

When we arrive in Paris he insists on taking me to the door of the Chevalier residence in Choisy-le-Roi. "I hope we meet again soon, Mademoiselle Aglaia," he murmurs as he bends over my hand and deposits a lingering kiss on it. Regretfully I think how infinitesimally small, if not non-existing, the chances are of that ever, ever happening.

I also think that Simon could learn a thing or two from him!

Monique and I both weep when I tell her about my father's last days, and then, in strictest confidence, I recount everything else that has happened. "I've had the ring with me ever since I found it", I tell her as I pull it out from under my blouse. "I hope it will help me find my family - that is, *if* I have one."

At first, she is speechless and keeps hugging me. Then she looks at the ring more closely and exclaims, "Aglaia, what if those bandits had really attacked? I mean what if they had robbed you of everything you have in the way of proof?"

"I know, I know. I didn't think of it at the time, but you can be sure I'll be thinking about nothing else from now on! I'll be very careful. Besides, I know how to defend myself: I forgot to tell you that I hit one of them on his arm with a cane. So hard that he kept hollering "bloody 'ell, she broke me arm!"

Monique shakes her head, then laughs out loud, "Yes, that sounds like you!" She hugs me, but frowns suddenly. "Wait a moment - the bandits spoke *English? In the middle of France?* Doesn't that strike you as odd?"

I hadn't thought of that at all, before, but as soon as Monique mentions it I agree. It is strange, but then I think - why wouldn't robbers move around like other people, from place to place, from country to country?

We talk about this some more and Monique agrees. "In a way it makes sense; it might be tempting fate far too much to 'work' the same places too often ... well, it's over and done with." We talk deep into the night, the way we always used to.

When she falls asleep, though, I am still awake with a strange new restlessness. Nerves? I try to think about the highwaymen calmly, logically, and come to the conclusion that they could not have been very experienced. Not that I am an expert on the subject, of course, but it must have been a random attack, the way it unfortunately still happens these days - at least according to Mr. Harwood. He maintains that an expanded French railroad net will result in less coach traffic; that therefore 'out-of-work' robbers will be forced to find other occupations, hopefully more legitimate ones. We had both laughed at that and again I think how pleasant a travel companion he had been the rest of the way.

I spend a week in Paris which I enjoy thoroughly. On my last day Jean-Philippe who has only recently become engaged tears himself away from his Sylvie and takes us on another tour of the city. Only a few monuments, he promises. I could have stayed much longer under the dark-blue gold-starred sky of the Sainte Chapelle dome, where it is easy to forget how overwhelmingly big, busy and noisy Paris is, but he is anxious to revisit Napoleon's tomb, opened to the public only very recently. 'Napoleon died on St. Helena in 1821 and was given a state funeral in 1840; his tomb was finished some twenty years later', he lectures us pompously. Monique and I nod politely and decide to admire the Church of the Dome from the outside, sitting on a park bench. I am not an admirer of Napoleon who, Father maintained, had plunged Europe into terrible and costly wars for more than twenty years. In the interest of fairness he would also mention that Napoleon's engineers had widened the Simplon Road between Brig and Domodossola which up to then had been little more than a mule track - not in order to ease local commerce, of course, but because he needed to move artillery equipment north.

Well, Jean-Philippe rattles off Napoleon's victories so often and in such detail that Monique implores him, 'No more!' She assures him that she has committed all of them to memory. He then turns to me and I tell him that I am satisfied remembering only the battle of the three Emperors at Austerlitz (Napoleon, Austrian Emperor Francis II and Czar Alexander I) because I have some slight difficulty remembering many dates. Naturally that elicits a grinning 'only slight?' from Monique. "Well, when was it?" her brother persists as I knew he would. I explain that, being ten years before Waterloo, remembering 1805 is easy. Jean-Philippe's dark look tells me that he considers me a traitor to his hero's memory.

Looking back I realize that the time I spent with Monique and her family has been very good for me. Being with her has helped me to get up in the morning and to look forward to what the new day will bring.

The train ride out of Paris, my very first one, is an exhilarating experience in spite of seats which I decide must be of the hardest wood; not only that, they are covered by the thinnest upholstery fabric imaginable. The trains are very fast: they are said to cover twenty miles an hour! Twenty miles! What I did not expect is the deafening noise they produce, even with all windows closed. If they are left only partially open, not only steam and soot pour into the compartments but engine sparks which are far more dangerous: they burn holes into your clothes before you are aware of what is happening!

Naturally there is not much to see through closed windows which get dirtier and dirtier. I only remember rows of poplars which Jean-Philippe says are typical of France. Apart from that he sits silently across from me, dreaming of his Sylvie, I suppose.

My first look at the English Channel filled me with awe - I had never seen a body of water larger than Lake Geneva. But this - this stretches out as far as the eye can see! And what hustle and bustle: boats of every shape and size are being loaded and unloaded, fishermen auction off their catches from their boats, women in striking costumes and white, frilly caps offer delicate lace to passengers, barefoot small boys dart in and out of the crowd. The babble of different languages fills the air – and speaking of air: it reeks not only of fish! Over by a dockside tavern a brawl had broken out which is encouraged and watched by a growing ring of spectators - and suddenly I have the eerie sensation that I am being watched, too. As nonchalantly as I can I look around but do not see anyone or anything suspicious. Get rid of those nerves, I tell myself as we walk the short distance to the Inn; that is no way to start on a journey. Jean-Philippe escorts me to the door of my second-floor room which commands a spectacular view of the harbor.

I open the window. It is getting cooler; the afternoon sky is changing from blue to grey, a sudden wind drives the clouds, masses them, tears them apart, reshapes them. After watching for a while how the wind whips up the waves and how quickly rain empties the pier of people I am about to close the window when I notice two men. The only ones left, they seem oblivious to the weather. The man wearing that dark cape - doesn't he look like Mr. Harwood? But he is talking - surely he is not one of 'our' bandits? Same stature, same torn clothing, but no kerchief covering his face, of course – by now the rain is coming down too hard to see anything. I must have imagined the resemblance.

The next morning, one day before our departure from France, the rain has abated but not the wind. I venture out anyway. I have to stop seeing people and things which aren't there! There are no dangers lurking around every corner and behind every tree! After about half an hour I find the rutted road with its water-filled holes and cracks and mud too slippery and the wind which keeps dislodging my bonnet so annoying that I decide to turn back. I take shelter against the Inn wall to retie my bonnet and continue on my way. I have taken not more than four or five steps towards the entrance when a loud crash to my rear startles me - I whip around and stare at the remains of a stone urn which has smashed itself into a hundred pieces. *On the very spot where I had been standing seconds ago!* Weakly I lean against the wall until the thought explodes in my mind, 'Why am I still standing here? Waiting for another urn to come down?' I rush inside and up to my room and bolt the door.

The maid has been in during my absence to leave a note from Jean-Philippe. Still shaken I sit down to read it. He apologizes that pressing business in London requires him to leave sooner and that he has been able to secure only his own passage on the earlier steamer. He suggests I join an English couple, Mr. and Mrs. Shadwell, who assured him that they will be glad to look out for me. He leaves instructions on getting to London from Dover and an address where he can be reached.

Well, I shall have to get along without him - not that I relish the idea. I think about the urn again. Gale-force winds could dislodge an urn, why not, especially if it is placed too close to the edge, or if it hasn't been properly secured, or if it is not secured at all. One had come down from the inn's roof garden, right where I had been standing ... why should that be cause for alarm? Did anyone know I was going to be standing on that very spot? Of course not, and that includes me. I have to stop making something of what was a mere coincidence. An even better idea: I am going to forget about coincidences altogether and look forward to my first steamer experience instead!

I am amazed at "Dieppe", our paddle steamer, and watch how the pistons pump back and forth, back and forth, while the huge red paddle wheels revolve and spray water in the air, but when we start to move the swaying motion and the strong odor of machine oil soon get the better of me. I hope that remaining up on top, taking deep breaths of the bracing sea air, leaning against the railing and looking at anything but the ceaseless shifting up-and-down of the horizon will help. It does not. Nothing helps.

We are in our fourth and last hour of crossing (I would never have survived a 'pre-steamer' crossing which took twice that long!), when Mr. Harwood chooses that very moment to come strolling down the deck. So he is here, too. Isn't that ... the thought disappears into the next wave of nausea. When he offers his assistance I manage a weak 'no, thank you' through clenched teeth and flee to my cabin. Seasickness is an affliction best borne in private.

I am as weak as a day-old kitten when we arrive in Dover, and again Mr. Harwood is there, offering a supporting arm as we go ashore. He leads me to the Inn where he leaves me to the ministrations of a chamber maid. One look at my presumably still gooseberry-greenish face is enough: she bundles me into bed and brings me a cup of strong tea and plain toast. Food and drink change nothing. Bed, chair, lamp, ceiling, walls – everything moves, even with my eyes closed.

I awake in the morning a new and very hungry person. There are trains to London, but my arrangements call for coach travel. Mr. Harwood pronounces himself delighted at my quick recovery and offers to telegraph ahead to the Langham Hotel on Portland Square and confirm my lodging arrangements. He tells me the Shadwells are staying there, too. He certainly knows how to find out much of what is happening ...

He is there to see me into the very large coach. He kisses my hand again and takes his leave, murmuring how devastated he is that our paths are unlikely to cross again since he has to remain in London, whereas I ...? He leaves the sentence dangling and me with the distinct impression that he is waiting for me to tell him my plans. I don't, but as soon as he is gone wish I had. I have promised to be careful - what harm could there have been in telling him?

The coach service to London starts out at an incredible speed while Mr. Shadwell holds forth about the lighthouse in Dover, the first one to be electrified, in 1858 he said, and look at it, isn't it a marvel? He intends to take his first ride on the London Underground the next day while the wife is shopping because he collects 'firsts!' He shakes his head at Lord Palmerston, the Prime Minister, who apparently refused an invitation to ride the inaugural train because at seventy-nine years of age he prefers to stay above ground as long as possible. I think this a clever and amusing answer, but Mrs. Shadwell, most likely having had to listen to the story once too often, sends a withering glance at her husband. There is no further mention of the Underground.

The countryside flies by, flat and green, bisected by hedges and dotted with thatched-roof cottages. It changes as we get closer to the city and not for the better. Soon my impression is one of indescribable filth and a terrible odor seeps into the coach. Is this really part of London? The houses are small, dilapidated, smoke-grimed and lean against each other in narrow streets. Sweepers clad in rags push piles of debris and refuse from one side of the street to the other. Water from a recent rain stands in deep puddles and is sprayed in all directions by our wheels. Traffic is appalling – I have never seen such a congestion of people and vehicles! Our coach has slowed to a snail's pace, vying for space with hansom cabs, horse-drawn omnibuses, carrier wagons, street traders. From the very beginning the air inside the coach has left much to be desired, but now an even more disagreeable odor invades the interior. Mrs. Shadwell awakes from her genteel-snore-accompanied nap and quickly withdraws two cologne-water-scented handkerchiefs from her reticule. She hands me one, saying, "We must be getting near the Thames, my dear; I knew you wouldn't be prepared." I rush to do as she does and bury my nose in the handkerchief, but when we reach a bridge curiosity gets the better of me and I crane for a closer look. Immediately I wish I hadn't. My stomach somersaults at the sight of the slimy, stagnant water that is filled with all manner of indescribable trash and filth - it bears no resemblance to the clear brooks and rivers I know. But of course this is a much larger, wider river.

Conditions improve once we are across the bridge and arrive in an area called Charing Cross. Traffic is still heavy, but now it moves on wider streets lined with stately homes, substantial buildings and shops. The size of the city is overwhelming. When we get off, Mr. Shadwell commandeers a hansom cab and soon the three of us are on our way to our hotel. During the ride Mrs. Shadwell regales me with the tale of the miraculous results her immersion in the Leukerbad thermals baths have produced against her stubborn arthritis and several 'internal' afflictions whose names she whispers to me behind her hand in such low tones that I cannot make out what they are, but I nod in sympathy.

"You're from somewhere near Leukerbad, aren't you? Do you know how hot that water is? Not everybody can take it," she announces proudly, "although I understand some guests spend hours and hours sitting in it!"

"I know it is about fifty degrees or thereabouts before it feeds into several pools. Of course that is fifty degrees Celsius," I tell her. In Brig everyone knows that these thermal baths have been in use since pre-Roman times. Father used to send patients there if they could afford it and sometimes made arrangements for the ones who could not ...

"Celsius, is that what it is called? Why can't they use British thermometers?" Disapproval coats her voice. "None of the measurements and scales in your country are like ours, not even the money – they really ought to change to our British ways. It would be so much more convenient for us travelers. There were people at the baths from Germany and France, even a family from Poland, or was it Bulgaria, maybe Hungary - well, just think how much money we spend in your country!"

I hope that she is done with the thermal baths, and indeed she is and immediately starts on a new subject. "By the way, we're staying only two nights at the Langham. Tomorrow morning I shop for clothes. You are welcome to accompany me if you like. If you don't mind my saying so, you could use something more ... fashionable?" Having dismissed my travel outfit she continues, "Day after, on the way home, we take the train to York to visit our daughter. She is married to a judge."

I could have sworn that her ample bosom swelled on the word 'judge' and quickly nod my appreciation. Although I dislike the arrogance of her thinking that the world ought to adopt "our British way of doing things," I am relieved when she announces, "Of course you'll dine with us tonight, my dear; this afternoon I must rest." It is kind of her to ask me. I had worried about how to handle having my first meal in an elegant hotel dining room on my own.

The Langham is *six* stories high and far more imposing

than I dreamed. Watching fashionably dressed ladies and couples glide in and out of the hotel with such self-assurance while we wait for our room assignments, I feel very provincial indeed and wonder whether Sir Arthur could steer me to less expensive quarters - or set me on my way to Cornwall right away which would decidedly be my preference when I am shown to my room: it can only be described as awash in gilded-velvety-tasseled splendor.

I spend the remainder of the afternoon making use of my luxurious bathroom (according to Mrs. Shadwell this unique innovation is found only in the very finest hotels), re-reading Mr. Dickens' Omnibus article and writing letters to Monique and Olga who, I'm sure, are concerned about me. There is not much to report, so I describe the malodorous (I have always wanted to use that word!) Thames and some of the 'extreme' fashions I have seen in the hotel lobby and add that I am looking forward to buying some new clothes. Nothing extreme of course, but also nothing black as tradition demands it. Father did not want me to wear black after Mother died which caused raised eyebrows among some of her friends. That is probably why I now believe, as he did, that mourning has nothing to do with the color one does or does not wear. How I wish he were here with me ...

My first hotel dinner – what can I say? Courses keep appearing, endlessly it seems. To mention only a few: oxtail soup followed by broiled mutton, mashed potatoes, peas and carrots; boiled fowl (I want to ask Mrs. Shadwell what kind of bird but don't, there is too little meat on its tiny bones to make it an interesting bird) with vegetables called Brussels sprouts which look and smell and taste like miniature cabbages (boiled into oblivion, Father would have commented!); all that was to be followed by woodcocks or partridges and more, all of which I politely refuse because I am curious about 'Canary Steamed Pudding', never having heard of steamed puddings before. It arrives, lemony and indeed canary-yellow, tasty if a bit soggy. After that I thank the Shadwells and go up to my room.

The following morning Mrs. Shadwell takes me under her wing and precedes me into Robinson's after explaining that it is a recently opened emporium which offers an excellent selection of quality clothes at prices which are not exorbitant. I suppose it all depends on one's understanding of exorbitant, but I have made up my mind not to let myself be intimidated which is easier said than done. However, once the saleswoman assigned to me realizes that I intend to purchase several outfits which are to be sent to the Langham ('you did say the Hotel Langham on Regent Street, Miss?') her condescending manner turns into fawning solicitude. For the first time in my life cost does not determine what I purchase: I enjoy myself selecting a navy-blue plaid walking dress with a spencer and a bonnet, two poplin dresses trimmed in velvet with matching three-quarter coats and veiled hats, some odds and ends - and I cannot resist a cream-colored evening gown embellished with tiny rosebuds and the prettiest slashed puff sleeves, not that I try to resist very hard! I have no idea when I might wear it ... dancing the night away with Mr. Harwood would have been nice, very nice indeed ...

I say good-bye and thank Mrs. Shadwell; she is returning to the hotel for a well-deserved rest while I am going to find my way to Sir Arthur's office. I have memorized the address and directions. Seeing how tightly passengers are packed into the horse-drawn omnibuses, exactly as Charles Dickens has described it, I am afraid of getting on and not being able to push my way off in time. What if I wind up at some God-forsaken end-of-the-line place outside of London? I'd never find my way back.

I decide to walk. It should take not more than twenty minutes. Of course it takes me only *one* of those minutes to realize that ladies do not walk about unattended: they are driven wherever they need or want to go. Well, it is too late to worry about that now, I am nearly there. I tighten the grip on my reticule. All I have to do is cross the street.

I am about to do that, along with a great many other people, when an omnibus draws up in front of us. I try to step back, but a vicious shove to my back sends me stumbling towards the horses; unable to regain my balance and duck out of the way, I already see myself falling under those thrashing hooves and being trampled to death and I'll never find out anything about my family ... but then, at the very last moment, I am yanked back by my coat sleeve. Someone has pushed me, hard, I am sure of that, but someone has pulled me back to safety. I manage to regain my balance. No one is taking the slightest notice of what so nearly happened.

Shaken and more frightened than I have ever been I slowly turn around. One of those street boys I have seen everywhere grins uncertainly at me before he lets go of my sleeve. He mumbles something I don't understand.

"D-did ... did you see who pushed me?" I can scarcely speak.

"Nae." He shakes his head.

I look at my unlikely rescuer who is maybe ten or eleven years old, stick-thin, and encrusted with blackish grime from his head to his bare feet. Who stands there, waiting. Of course! Tightening the grip on my reticule I pull a shilling out of it and hand it to him, resisting the strong urge to wipe my hand after he palms it. He disappears into the crowd before I can say anything.

Shaken, I manage to cross the street with the crowd without further mishap, but I have lost my taste for walking around London. I feel the stirrings of homesickness for the clean air of our mountains, the openness, the quiet and the people I have left behind. I cannot help looking over my shoulder, every now and then, uneasy about my narrow escape. I have dismissed the urn as mere coincidence, but this, coming so soon after the urn, makes me wonder whether the two events could be connected?

Ridiculous! Being jostled in a crowd, especially in a large city, must be a daily if not hourly occurrence. Except ... except for the fact that the push to my back had been hard and well-aimed, hard enough for me to feel and believe that it had been deliberate.

I keep walking, alert to my surroundings, and in order to regain some calm I try to line up the facts as I know them. *Fact one*: I don't know anyone in London. True. *Fact two*: No one in London knows me. Also true. Fact *three*: No one knows *why* I am here. Also true. *Fact four*: There is no number four - unless I count getting more and more annoyed at myself. Also true. What will I do next? Come over faint? Give in to the jim-jams? Let myself be taken by the vapors?

No!

Chapter VIII

Doubly vigilant I continue on my way and am greatly relieved when I find myself in front Sir Arthur's building. The doorman ushers me in and directs me to the third floor, second door to the left. The gaslights flickering on the landings and in the corridors make it easy to find the office. When no one reacts to my knocking I knock again, more forcefully this time, and enter a large room. Four men, working at standing desks, ignore me. The one nearest to the door, younger than the others, eventually looks up from a ledger.

I ask to see Sir Arthur.

"I presume you have an appointment?"

Why didn't I arrange for one? Well, I hardly had time to do that, but I ought to have remembered that Sir Arthur is not Uncle Kaspar. "Not an appointment exactly," I answer, "but Sir Arthur ..."

" ... doesn't see anybody without appointment!" he finishes my sentence in a haughty voice, managing to convey that only people of diminished mental capacity could be unaware of this. His attention is back on his ledger before he has finished speaking.

"Sir Arthur is expecting me as soon as I arrive in London. That is what I was trying to tell you!" I have raised my voice; I am prepared to raise it further if it becomes necessary. At that very moment another door opens. A tall gentleman enters, papers in hand, and inquires what the commotion is all about.

Before anyone can start explaining, he takes one look at me, nods and turns towards his clerks. "Miss Andereggen is to be admitted immediately, at any time," he says severely, without raising his voice. "All of you: that is an order!" He leads me into another room while the four outdo each other, nodding and respectfully repeating, "Yes, Sir, certainly Sir, yes Sir."

"I have been expecting you," he continues, indicating a chair. "Welcome to London. I trust you had a smooth and pleasant journey?"

Feeling as if a heavy burden had been lifted off my shoulders, I sink into one of the leather armchairs. Sir Arthur looks just like Uncle Kaspar had described him, tall and bookish and with a gleam in his eyes – Father would have liked him ...

His question, however, reminds me of what so nearly happened not even half an hour earlier. Something must have shown on my face.

"There is nothing amiss, is there?" he asks.

"I am not sure ... what I mean to say is that I don't know what to make of something that happened earlier this afternoon. Someone tried to push me under an omnibus."

Sir Arthur sits up. "Good Heavens, what are you saying? Are you certain?"

"If you mean did I see the person who pushed me? No, I didn't, but I know I was pushed. It was a very hard shove."

"It couldn't have been the crowd moving forward, being jostled?"

"No, it wasn't like that at all. It was a push, a very hard push. To the middle of my back. I'm sure of that, and so is the boy who grabbed me by my coat sleeve and managed to pull me back just in time."

While I wait for Sir Arthur to think about this I look around his well-appointed office, taking in the many books, the framed hunting prints, the enormous mahogany desk with its silver ink stand. Everything looks very substantial and somehow that feels comforting. He seems to be a little older than Uncle Kaspar, has a keen, intelligent look about him which, combined with an air of kindness and humor, reminds me of Father.

"Well, we may never know exactly what happened there, so let's leave that for the time being and get to the reason you came to London, shall we? First let me express my condolences on the death of your father ... my friend Kaspar has already informed me that you are searching for your family, and has explained why," he said. "Who is aware of your search, as far as you know?"

"Only my best friend, Monique Chevalier, who lives in Paris with her family. Olga, our housekeeper knows, but she is really a member of the family. Of course Simon Riedmatten knows, the doctor who is ... who was my father's partner."

"I see." He reaches for pen and paper. "What say we get started? Let's examine what we have. Or rather what we don't have. To the best of my knowledge and from what Kaspar wrote, there are no identity papers, documents, no marriage license, birth certificate or other records ... all we have is the copy Kaspar made of your father's notebook, or letter, which is now under lock and key in my office. Correct?"

I nod.

"And there is some jewelry?"

Again I nod. "I didn't bring the pearls, they are beautiful but just pearls. I always wear my locket, but I also have the ring and the two miniatures with me." I disengage the ring from my necklace and slide everything towards him.

Sir Arthur examines the likenesses first, using a

magnification glass and looking back and forth between them and me. "Yes, it is easy to see a resemblance. Of course these are small portraits, and as you surely are already aware of, resemblance is not accepted as proof in a court of law. Establishing and verifying the identities of these two people will not be easy, not having names and dates and places to start with ..."

Seeing my worried look he assures me that by 'not easy' he in no way means 'impossible'. "We also must try to establish ownership of the miniatures and jewelry back to your father, your British father. The fact that they were found in the coach involved in the accident does not of itself prove that he is their rightful owner."

I had never thought of that. I wonder how many other things I haven't thought of ...

Sir Arthur picks up the ring. "What a striking piece," he says and walks over to a smaller desk on which stands a lamp which disburses a very powerful light. He examines the ring from all sides. "I've seen similar gold rounds on a black background before, can't think for the moment what they are called," he said. "You usually wear it around your neck?"

I nod. "Yes, on my locket chain. Always *under* my blouse, of course. The chain is solid and has a good catch."

"I am glad to hear that. However, there are safer places to keep important items, especially in view of what nearly happened this morning. My clients keep their valuables at a bank not far from here. I'd like you to accompany me there, be introduced to the manager who will witness your belongings being put into a safe. You will also leave your signature on record; that will grant you access to them and to your account as well in the future."

I think this sounds needlessly complicated, and as if he could read my mind Sir Arthur says, "I cannot impress on you strongly enough the need for caution and secrecy. At this time we have no way of knowing whether other people, *unbeknownst to you*, know of your search. We don't know where this may lead, whom or what you may encounter - so let's start by going to the bank. Keep the locket, of course, as long as you wear it hidden from view."

I cannot think of a compelling reason why I wouldn't go along with his suggestions, so that's what we do, without having to wait at all to be attended to. Obviously Sir Arthur is well known there. On our way out he asks whether I am satisfied and comfortable with my lodging.

"Almost too comfortable," I answer. "Everything is ... too, too ... ." I cannot find a word to adequately describe the grandeur of the Latham.

"Too opulent, too rich - is that what you are trying to say?"

"Yes, opulent is *the* perfect word for the Langham."

"Yes, it is that. This being the case, would you like

me to arrange to have your things moved to a less pretentious place? You may have to remain in London for some time." He thinks for a moment. "I could recommend to the Alford. Very comfortable, and only a few streets from my residence and this office."

Of course I agree. Sir Arthur arranges for his man Henry to call for me at eleven the next day. Before he sees me into a hansom cab, he again makes me promise to wear the locket inside my blouse at all times in a compromise for not wanting to keep it in a bank safe. He waves away my thanks and my awkward inquiry about his fee, saying only, "Let's discuss that when I have some answers for you. Meanwhile - let me compliment you on your excellent command of English."

What a surprise, Mr. Thornton was good for something after all! I realize that I am getting used to speaking English. Father was right!

I feel relieved of a heavy burden, having left the search for my family in Sir Arthur's capable hands. But along with that comes the realization of how naïve I have been not anticipating difficulties: I had never thought that others might be aware about my search; in a way I still don't see how that is possible ...

Back at the Langham, I bathe and try on all my new outfits again - and feel that I look very grown up and very pretty in them! After I have treated myself to tea and cakes I decide to take a walk on the hotel promenade, secure in the knowledge that now I can hold my own against most of the elegant ladies! As I am nearing the corner, I see one of the hotel porters trying to shoo away a boy with a broom, shouting and gesturing at him to be off. When he sees me he apologizes for the "presence of the likes of him" so near the hotel and threateningly raises his broom again.

"Don't do that, please, let him be!" I say to him, politely but firmly. I have come close enough to see that the boy is *the* boy. He stands defiant, with both thin arms raised protectively around his head and peers up at me. One eye is puffy and bruised; there is a cut on his forehead.

"Did he do that to you?" I ask.

"Nae, t'weren't *'im!*" his answer comes quickly. "T'were the bloke wot takes me shillin'. Takes it n' sez nex' time 'e sees me 'e ..." He draws a hand across this throat to make sure I understand.

"*What?* Who said that?"

"Dunno 'is name."

I have trouble understanding him, what with all the dropped 't's and 'h's, and also absorbing what all of this means, but then another thought strikes me.

"How did you find me?"

"Huh?"

I repeat the question.

"Follerd ye," he shrugs, as if it had been the simplest thing in the world. He must have run after my hansom cab the entire way.

"Why?"

He shrugs again. Hoping to see me again, hoping I might replace the shilling? While I am thinking about what to do, this thin, filthy boy to whom I owe a great deal more than replacing a shilling stands waiting patiently in front of me. He does not ask for anything.

"Where do you live?" I ask him.

"Aw, 'ere n' ere."

"Don't you have a family?"

He shakes his head 'no'.

"Nobody at all?"

"I done tole ye: no fambly!"

"That is the truth?"

"I does awright fer meself!" he says defiantly and turns to go. "Ain't lyin'!" he adds over his shoulder.

"Wait, wait - I believe you, but where do you go at night? I mean, where do you sleep?"

He looks at me, dumbfounded that I need to ask.

"Where?"

"Railroad arches, under tarps what cover wagons n' barges n'such," he explains impatiently, "jest a place wot's dry".

An idea is taking shape in my mind during his explanation.

"Listen, you got that black eye and those bruises because you helped me, isn't that right?"

He nods in agreement.

"It's only fair that I do something for you. Come with me."

I ignore his reluctance which disappears as soon as I mention 'food'. He even lets me grab him by his grubby-sticky hand. Together we march back to the hotel entrance. Past the disbelieving doorman, past two head-shaking reception managers who are too shocked to try to stop us - after all I *am* a paying guest here - past scandalized ladies tut-tutting behind gloved hands. I haul him up to my room and ring for the maid, order up lots of hot water and extra towels, dinner for two, and pressing some coins into her hand ask her to see about some used clothes for him: the Langham's widely advertised claim that they could provide absolutely *everything* for their valued guests is about to be put to the test. Then I cross my fingers.

"What do they call you?" I ask.

He is too intent on seeing and absorbing everything there is to see in my room to answer. He wants to know how many people sleep in the very large, very ornate bed which is piled high with pillows; he does not believe me when I answer, "one" and point to myself. I ask for his name again.

"Ben."

"Ben what?"

He shrugs. "Jes' Ben."

"All right, JustBen, let's see about that cut now."

He is slippery and manages to evade my grasp several times. Fortunately hot water and food arrive soon and at the same time – his eyes grow big when the tempting aromas of our dinners waft over to him. Treatment for the cut will have to wait.

"We wash our hands before we eat." Father could always tell when I tried to get around his rule, but was angry only the one time when I lied about having washed them. I pull JustBen over to the wash basin. He copies what I do, then sits down at the table. I heap his plate with boiled chicken, potatoes and carrots and he digs into the food with both hands before I can point to the knife and fork lying next to his plate. When he notices that I use mine he announces, speaking through a mouth full of chicken, "Don't 'old wiv' dose, Miss."

"Try them out at breakfast tomorrow, if you like."

He stops shoveling food into his mouth. "Nae, I cain't stay 'ere!"

"Why not? It'll be dark by the time I take care of your eye and that cut."

"So?" he says, tempted but suspicious. " 'Ow d' yer know wot ter do, wiv me eye n'such?"

"My father is ... he was a doctor."

"Ye learn from 'im?"

It is stretching the truth a bit, but I nod. He methodically finishes eating. After I motion to go ahead, he scrapes what is still clinging to the serving pieces onto his plate. He has put away a meal that would set up a grown man for a day.

My next task is to assure him that bathing tubs are not an invention of the Devil and that no, the drain will not suddenly grow bigger and swallow him! I warn him to keep the soap out of his eyes and promise to avert my eyes but insist on washing his hair - obviously his head has had no acquaintance with soap and water for a very long time, and I have no desire to acquire tiny creepy-crawly beasties! I wash and rewash his hair three times, then apply salve to his cuts and bruises. The maid brings in a change of clothing, slightly too large but clean, and a pair of used boots which, miraculously, are the right size and which he cannot stop admiring and touching.

There are even socks and a sleep shirt. Over his loud protests she takes away his smelly rags, pinched between two fingers and held as far away from her person as her arm will reach.

Ben has become very quiet. His hair, lighter by several shades of brown, keeps falling over his forehead and into his eyes and he impatiently pushes it out of the way. I ask if he would like me to trim it. He nods eagerly. "Jes' 'nough so's I c'n bloody see, Miss!" He returns from checking out his haircut in the bathroom mirror, looking pleased. "Better, innit?"

"Much better. How about your fingernails?"

He refuses my scissors. "Nae, Miss, do 'em mesef."

I cannot imagine how and what with, but I have other, more pressing questions to ask him. He figures that he is twelve or thereabouts, has been on his own for years, doesn't rightly know how many, but remembers begging on the streets when he were real small. His Mum was very sick 'after the new baby, but it died when it were tiny'. Then his Mum died, too; he don't know his Da.' Where does he sleep? "I done tole ye 'fore," he says impatiently. He talks about everything in a matter-of-fact tone, taking life as it happens, uncomplaining. He does not expect anything different, anything better. This is all he knows.

I put two pillows and a blanket on the chaise lounge and watch him squirm into a comfortable position. He

falls asleep very quickly and doesn't look so tough anymore – but what am I going to do with him? What if
he turns out to be a bad pear? The thought makes me
smile: Olga stubbornly says 'bad pear' instead of 'bad
apple', no matter how often we point out that she is
mixing up her fruits.

All at once I cannot keep my eyes open any longer
either, but still new questions race around in my head:
Who pushed me? Why? And as always the one question for which there is no answer spirals away from the
others and torments me: why did Father ride up to the
old mill that night? Did someone make him go there?
Who? Why?

Sir Arthur's Henry arrives promptly at eleven. If he is
surprised by the presence of a boy who is wearing clothing a size too large and sports a black eye, he does not
show it. Earlier, I gave JustBen who likes his new name a
choice: he is free to go, whenever he chooses, or he can
stay with me for the time being and 'eat regular' - 'for the
time being', I explain to him, meaning for as long as I am
in London, which could be days or weeks, but probably
not longer. He again declines the loan of my nail scissors
and bites down a couple of fingernails while he thinks.
He announces that he will stick around, "for a day, meb-
be two, Miss." I understand: he is doing me a favor.

Henry sees us settled and tells me to expect Sir
Arthur around five. I know right away that the Alford is

a much better place for us. In my new cozy room I soon have the pleasure of watching JustBen devour the food I had sent up, this time wrestling with eating utensils, without needing to be reminded. He learns quickly ... having a younger brother must be somewhat like this ... the thought sets me to wondering whether I have family, aunts and uncles, cousins, what they might be like ...

Later, JustBen asks whether we could go outside. Of course we can; I am not letting a near accident turn me into a recluse! We go across to a small park and it is heavenly, being away from the noise and dirt and discovering the pleasures of this pretty, treed expanse of green.

So far I have detected no 'bad pear' signs.

Sir Arthur is already at the hotel when we return. JustBen rudely ignores his greeting and regards him with suspicion. I explain that I have some private business to discuss with the gentleman. Looking angry and baffled JustBen shoulders past Sir Arthur and storms out of the hotel.

Sir Arthur holds me back, "Let him go. May I ask how or why you 'acquired' him?" He is disturbed when I give him a full accounting of the 'attack' and several times repeats the need for caution. He also questions the wisdom of being side-tracked by JustBen's problems instead of concentrating on my own affairs. "And give some thought to this: it might be kinder, in the long run, to let him go before he becomes used to a life he can never hope to have," he adds. "Now shall we get to your affairs?"

"You have news?" I am barely able to contain my impatience.

"I do, as a matter of fact!" He looks very pleased with himself, but looking at my face he launches into a lecture about drawing premature conclusions from any information he has obtained so far. Just like Uncle Kaspar - is caution *always* uppermost in a lawyer's mind?

"As luck would have it," he finally comes to the point, "I dined last night with an old friend who may be in a position to help us. He is a well-known authority on genealogy and heraldry."

"And?"

"And please don't let yourself be carried away! He remembered seeing a design similar to the one on your locket and the ring that he believes *may be* associated with a Cornwall family; he agrees that Cornwall would be a logical place to start our investigation, especially after I mentioned the two pamphlets that were with your father's notebook. Incidentally, Harringtons used to live in Cornwall, a long time ago."

"What else did he say?"

"I am repeating what he said to me: this does not necessarily mean that you have family living there, or anywhere else in England. People move about, for a variety of reasons. We have to start by examining Cornish records, Parrish registers, deeds, sales, records of legal proceedings, etc. etc. Naturally, this will take time."

He obviously expects a reaction from me, but all I can think of is, "Cornish? Meaning from ... ?"

"From Cornwall, yes," he explains, "which is about some 250 miles southwest of London. As I said before, there is a great deal to be looked into. You need to be patient. Let's wait and see what develops."

We have a beginning! And isn't it a good thing that Sir Arthur has no idea that 'wait and see' is something I don't do very well!

"Aglaia?"

"I understand, Sir, I do."

His gently insistent voice brings me back to the present. We sit and chat for a while. Since JustBen has not returned (I have gone outside several times to look) we eat dinner in the hotel. It is quite good but does not compare to Olga's knack of combining Hungarian and Valais fare!

After Sir Arthur leaves, I remain downstairs and write letters, but JustBen does not return.

He reappears in the morning, hungry but not the least little bit contrite. While he gulps down eggs, bacon and toast and washes everything down with tea - "don't like milk, never 'ad it" - I make clear to him that further dis-appearing acts will not be tolerated. "Either you stay with me while I am in London, or you leave now, for good," I say firmly although I don't want him to go. I am getting used to his company and I like him.

He stares at me with big eyes while he sops up the last of the eggs with the last of the toast, thinks for a while and mouth still full, asks, "Wot 'm I sposter do then?"

What indeed? "Well, what do you want to do?" I throw the question back at him.

"Learn a trade," he says, without a moment's hesitation.

"What sort of trade?"

"Dunno, wiv animals."

"I wonder if something could be arranged," I think out loud.

"Awr, go on!" His voice tells me that if *I* am dream-ing, *he* is not.

"No, let me think about this for a minute!" The more I think about it, the surer I am that he saved me from injury. He may even have saved my life. That push had caused me to lose my balance and if he hadn't grabbed my coat sleeve – I already saw myself stumbling into and under the horses' hooves, knowing that it was all over. I shall never forget that terrible feeling of helplessness, of inevitability. Perhaps, with Sir Arthur's help of course, something could be done about a trade that might give him a future - the least I owe him is to find out. If I don't, this city is going to swallow him the way it must swallow hundreds if not thousands of children who stay alive by begging, stealing and other ways I cannot begin to imagine! In only a few days I have seen so many, too many. How many do survive, I wonder?

"Finding out will take some time, but meanwhile" – the idea suddenly comes to me – "meanwhile, how would you like to learn how to read?"

"*Read?*" The word comes out a squeak. He looks at me as if I had gone quite mad.

"Yes, read," I repeat. "Street and store signs, newspapers, later when you know how even stories, perhaps entire books. Being able to read gives you an advantage for just about anything in life - *and in any trade, with or without animals.*" Thinking that he might not have understood 'advantage' I add, "I mean that being able to read is important for any trade, whatever you do." It would also give me something to do while stuck here in 'wait and see'.

"I dunno." He looks doubtful but tempted, if only by eating regular, and asks, "Anyways, who'd teach me?"

I point to myself with more assurance than I feel – how difficult could it be? In grade school I used to help Vreni and Renate with reading and arithmetic.

"Aright then, Miss," he shrugs. I know: he is doing me another favor.

It is a simple matter to procure a slate and chalks. By the afternoon he is squirming on a chair, writing and erasing letters and numbers, over and over and over again. Obviously he has figured out some letter combinations on his own in the streets. He is tenacious. Only the promise that he can practice outside with signs and house numbers entices him to quit.

And so the days pass, slowly - snail-like slowly.

He learns quickly and remembers with ease. His cuts and bruises heal and he even seems to be filling out a bit. He is a nice-looking boy, but no matter what I say, sees no need for "washin' 'ands what ain't real dirty." He becomes more talkative every day and wants to know where I lived before the hotel. When I try to describe our tall mountains whose tops are snow-covered even during summer, he shakes his head. "Aw, no, Miss, that cain't be right," and what he doesn't understand at all is that I left Barry behind. Neither does he believe that Saint Bernards are bred and trained to work in pairs and that they save people lost or stranded in snow storms - but he asks for these stories again and again.

Time creeps by, still snail-like slowly. Every night when I go to sleep I wonder if the new day will bring news. Sir Arthur leaves messages every few days. "Nothing to report yet. Be patient."

For how long?

It is nearly three long weeks before he comes to see me again. He moves as sedately as ever but cannot keep excitement from showing on his face. He knows something. We go into a quiet corner of the hotel's reading room; I sit, stand, sit down again and suddenly cannot speak.

"Yes, I have some news!" he says. "Sit, sit down, my dear. My friend was right about Cornwall. Not only was he right: he traced your ring to a family by the name of Trelawney. And by the way, there is an old Cornish saying: By the Tre, Ros, Car, Lan, Pol and Pen, Ye may know most Cornishmen". He pauses dramatically.

'That is very nice, but why do I have to know that?' I think and when I don't answer, he adds, "That makes Trelawney a good Cornish name."

"I see, yes. Trelawney," I try out the name. What matters to me is that my father W.J.T. has just become W.J. Trelawney, my mother T. Trelawney. It is a beginning, but how do we go about finding out their given names?

"What does he know about the family?"

"He discovered something which may be important. There are several branches; two are extinct and one immigrated to Ceylon decades ago, supposedly went into the tea growing business there. He expects to receive more detailed information about other branches before long."

I wonder what 'before long' means in the legal world and can hardly believe that finally, finally some information is forthcoming. Sir Arthur mistakes my sigh of relief for an expression of impatience and gives my hand a fatherly pat.

"Inquiries like yours cannot be rushed, my dear. On the contrary, they must be conducted with utmost discretion. I must also point out to you something you may not have thought of: the possibility that your sudden appearance may not be greeted with delight. As a matter of fact, that is more than likely if an inheritance is at stake."

I want to protest that my search has nothing to do with an inheritance but stop myself - I am the *only* person who knows that!

"Let me put it in a different way," Sir Arthur continues. "We need to gather all the information about the Trelawney family *before* you try to see them; we have to make sure that they are indeed *your* family. You must remember: they don't know you exist - what's more, they may even dislike the idea that you exist. For your own good, for your protection, you must be in possession of as many facts as possible before you present yourself on their doorstep."

I suppose that once again I have been naïve. I look up at Sir Arthur's kind, concerned face. He is doing his best by me, I know that, but isn't he worrying too much? I tell him that of course he is right, that I know he has my interests at heart, that I greatly appreciate everything he is doing for me. That seems to please him and he asks whether there is anything else he could do for me while we await further information.

JustBen - I ask about the possibility of apprenticing him to a trade.

"You have decided to keep the boy?" Sir Arthur does not seem pleased at all about the idea.

"He knows that it is only for the time being, but when I think of how far he has come with his reading with only me showing and teaching him ... he is intelligent and learns quickly; he should be given a chance to learn something. He is a good boy."

"Hm ..." Sir Arthur strokes his chin as he reflects on the new problem I have handed him. "Your thinking does you credit, Aglaia, but in no way are you responsible for the boy's future. You do know that, don't you?"

I cannot very well say, 'You are wrong, Sir, I *do* feel responsible for him', so I don't say anything and wait for what *he* is going to say next.

With a small shrug he finally says, "On the otherhand I am getting to know that determined look of you! know that determined looks of yours! I have given the matter some thought and know of a family where he could board while he attends a grammar school. That might be a solution for the time being ... you are well able to afford the twenty-five guineas or so a year ... he is what, about ten, eleven? Let me think about this some more, but by all means let's wait until your own situation is settled."

I thank him again and go upstairs, where JustBen is busy practicing his letters.

I have so much to think about, but always my thoughts find their way back to Father's accident and later to the initial "T". What could my mother's name have been? Every name I think of strikes me as stiff and formal or outlandish! Therese? There is always Thalia ... if *her* parents liked Greek mythology, but what is the chance of that!

As it happened, there is not much time to think.

Sir Arthur is back with more news only a few days later. "The telegraph is such an extraordinary invention," he says, beaming. "In the old days information out of Cornwall would have taken many days to reach London, but today it is received within minutes ... I asked my friend to telegraph his answer, seeing that your patience is wearing a wee bit thin." He smiles and shakes his head in mute admiration for this modern marvel while I sit on the proverbial pins and needles, waiting for his news.

"Well, Aglaia," he says at last, "I looks like my friend directed his inquiries to the proper branch of the Trelawney family."

"And ...?" Why doesn't he speak faster, come to the point?

"His agent, of course, did not speak to family members yet - however he did gather a very interesting piece of information: one Trelawney son, William John Trelawney, left Cornwall around 1845, possibly 1846, with his wife. They are believed to have spent some time in London before leaving for the Continent, possibly with an infant, but there has been *no news of them since then.*"

I let out the breath I had not been aware I had been holding during his recital. It fits, it fits, it all fits - he has found my father! "William John," I say slowly. "My father's name is William John Trelawney ... that is what you are telling me, isn't it?"

In his cautious, measured way Sir Arthur allows that, yes, that would be a reasonable assumption. Then he points to his arm which I have clutched in my excitement and am still holding on to. I stammer an apology as I let go but all he says is, "Think nothing of it, my dear."

I try to sort out the many questions that whirl around in my head. "Did he find out my mother's name?"

He shakes his head. "No, at least not yet. The complete lack of records and information about her and their marriage is rather unusual and might - remember I said might - might indicate that theirs was not a marriage well-received by one or both families. But let me tell you what we have been able to establish: There is a Mr. Trelawney, an elderly gentleman who resides at Trelawney Manor, near Mill Brook and not far from Saint Agnes."

"And he ... he is ... " Suddenly I am afraid to say it.

"William John Trelawney's father. He may very well be, which would make him ..."

"My grandfather!" If I were alone, I might just jump up and down with the excitement of it, but I have enough sense not to do that here.

"It would seem so."

Would seem so – may very well be - would make him: don't lawyers ever answer questions more clearly, more decidedly? If not with a 'certainly' or 'absolutely' - couldn't they sometimes give you a simple yes or no?

"Saint Agnes, by the way, is on Cornwall's north shore. I expect that more details will follow in due time."

I manage a 'thank you', but all I can think of is, 'I have a grandfather'. My mother's parents died very young, years before I was born, whenever that was, I still don't know - and I have only hazy but wonderful memories of my paternal grandfather, a ruddy-faced old man and wonderful story teller who always good-naturedly laughed when I wanted to touch, even pull his gray beard a little - not only that, he let me! He died before I was six ... but now I have another grandfather!

My thoughts jump to something else. "Trelawney Manor – I wonder, doesn't that sound like a grand place?"

Sir Arthur laughs. "Well, the Trelawney family do own mines. Mine owners used to build grand homes for themselves, vie with one another as to who could outdo the competition. It may very well be grand. You won't know until you see the house."

Another 'may very well be', but nothing can dampen my excitement now. What should I do first? What I would really like to do is leave for Cornwall immediately. No, first I must find out how to get there. No, first I have to finish making arrangements for JustBen, but then ...

Sir Arthur watches me, a concerned look on his face. "You are not thinking of rushing there on your own, are you?" he asks.

I suppose good lawyers either learn to interpret their client's reactions, or they are born mind-readers. The blush I feel creeping up over my face is all the answer he needs.

"Aglaia, I cannot advise strongly enough against hasty actions on your part," he says in his slow, deliberate way. "I shall draft a letter to Mr. Trelawney, after which ..."

"How can I wait for letters to go back and forth and back and forth again and again?" I interrupt him. "That will take forever and ..."

"And *I* regret to have to say this, Aglaia: for the first time since we have met you are behaving in an unreasonable, childish manner! There are many reasons why you should not appear at Trelawney Manor without proper introduction. First there is the possibility of ... I see you are not interested. Very well. In any event, you *must* wait for the rest of the information; a month ought to be sufficient. As I have already told you, I should be able to travel with you in a month's time, but not sooner ... I see that does not appeal to you, either." He shakes his head. "Aglaia, I do understand your impatience, but you must try to be more patient ... there might not be another JustBen to rush to your rescue should you, the Lord forbid, need one! I promised your Uncle Kaspar to look out for you and I take my promises seriously! Need I remind you of your near accident?"

"No, but I have been here for weeks and weeks and weeks - and nothing has happened! Nobody knows that I am here, nobody knows why I am here. I am beginning to think that near accident could have happened to anyone."

"That may be so, but the fact remains that it happened to *you* ... and the boy's beating after he came to your aid: was that a coincidence, too?"

"No, he doesn't like to talk about it, but he is sure it was an older and stronger boy, a bully who wanted to get 'is greedy 'ands on me shillin' is the way he puts it." Sir Arthur does not look convinced but in smooth lawyerly fashion segues into another subject.

"At least consider this: we only know of two sons, but there may be others. So far we know nothing at all about the second son, or any of the others, but I need to caution you that in my years of practice I have come across brothers, once the best of friends, who became bitter enemies over an inheritance. I have seen this happen more times than I like to recall. The surviving brother, or brothers, may be less than delighted at your sudden appearance."

When that doesn't provoke a reaction from me, he challenges me with, "Well, what about Ben – are you going to walk away from him?"

"No, I would never do that! He keeps saying that he wants to learn a trade - maybe with animals - and at the same time he tells me he is 'afeared' of school' because he doesn't know what it will be like – but if you can get him into that grammar school and board him in a good home I'll gladly pay the costs. We'll have to see how he fares there, of course. And I shall have to withdraw money for my own expenses."

Sir Arthur sighs before he makes one more attempt at getting me to see reason: "At least wait until a suitable travel companion can be found. I cannot stress strongly enough that *ladies* do not travel unattended."

That last pronouncement sounded exactly like one of Madame's! I tell him that I realize it is not the same, of course, but that I have traveled from Brig to Geneva and back again by myself for nearly four years, and that I am used to doing that. I pause for a moment before I add, surprising myself, "I should be very grateful if you can find someone to accompany me in three days' time, because that is when I hope to be on my way."

That leaves him speechless for a moment. "If you were my daughter, I would forbid you to go alone, forbid you!" he informs me. "Unfortunately I don't have the right to forbid you anything, more's the pity!" I know that he must be annoyed or angry, and yet there is no hint of it in his voice. Does he *ever* raise it, I wonder?

"I cannot prevent you from wearing your locket," he continues, "but ring and portraits stay in the bank vault until they are needed. No discussion." Suddenly he looks as if he were trying not to smile. "Three days, you say. Do you have any idea how long it has been since I was given an ultimatum? I can scarcely remember back that far. Well, well, well ... I suppose I had better have one of my clerks start on your travel arrangements and on Ben's school."

I thank him and he leaves, head-shaking and chuckling as he repeats 'Three days' to himself while I appreciate the fact that he did not stress the considerable difference between Brig-Geneva and London-Cornwall!

It takes only two days to make my travel arrangements and to see JustBen settled into Brower's Academy under his new name of Benjamin Smith. Sir Arthur and

I inspected the school. The boys looked healthy and clean and seemed reasonably happy which I suppose is as good a way to judge a school as any when you are pressed for time. Sir Arthur, I realize by now, is able to make many things happen just by mentioning his name. He has offered, God bless him, to take in Benjamin for the time being and waves away my thanks by saying that his usually dour, unflappable housekeeper has brightened at the prospect of her cooking putting some meat on a skinny young 'un's bones. When I am surprised that his household is quite small, he brushes that aside, adding only that yes, it used to be larger, but that this is what he is comfortable with at this stage in his life. I hope JustBen will behave and that the two will get along with each other ...

I wish Benjamin good luck and when we say goodbye he struggles over something he has trouble saying. I tell him not to worry, that we will see each other again.

"Aw, Miss, t'ain't that," he answers, but I am pretty sure that it was 'xactly that!

All that remains to be done is to write to Monique, Uncle Kaspar, Olga. Simon, too, although he has yet to answer one of my letters ...

And then it is time to be on my way.

Sir Arthur still disagrees strongly with what I am about to do. "Ladies do not travel alone," he repeats severely, as if it were a law, "you must think about your reputation." I assure him again that I do and always shall. He waves away my question about a fee and presents me with a sturdy hooded poplin coat of which, he explains, I will have great need where I am going, Cornwall being blessed with an inordinate amount of rain. "You have a trusting nature, Aglaia, promise to be on guard at all times," he impresses on me. "At all times. Telegraph the office if you need anything, or write if it is not very urgent. Write if you need anything, anything at all. Especially write to me if there should be any trouble along the way, or once you arrive - of course I shall write to Mr. Trelawney." He shakes his head after he helps me into the coach and walks away without looking back.

Chapter IX

So here I am, feeling very alone in a large coach filled to capacity.

It would be very far from the truth to say that I am at ease. I miss Sir Arthur's reassuring presence. I could have traveled from London to Redruth and from there on to Penzance by train which would have been faster, but I am not ready to put my trust in trains and to undertake changing from one to another on my own. Besides, I am used to the cheaper coach travel.

Sir Arthur's warning, "Be on guard at all times," rings not only in my ears but in my head. Hasty decisions have landed me in trouble in the past, but I am trying not to think about them. Here I am, confined with other travelers in a stuffy, uncomfortable vehicle for several days, concentrating on being *careful*.

To begin with, how can I be certain that my fellow travelers are who they pretend to be? That portly, middle-aged country squire with the beady black eyes under heavy eyebrows – how do I know that he is not a villain? The black-gowned, heavily veiled lady who nervously clutches and fingers the contents of the large velvet satchel on her lap and cannot look anyone in the eye, what is she planning - murder? I know that my imagination is running wild but I don't seem able to rein it in. That thin man who keeps cracking his knuckles – why is he so nervous, does he have evil on his mind, too? I even distrust the young mother whose fussy infant might be nothing but a clever ploy intended to remove suspicion from her own person! I sit stiffly alert and vigilant, at the same time feeling too, too ridiculous for words. Such weird imaginings are not like me!

To make matters worse the country squire now instructs us gleefully that, should we ever find ourselves in a runaway coach (which according to him happens frequently but is a possibility that had never entered my mind!), the best course of action is doing nothing. "That's right, ladies n' gentlemen, brace yerself 'cause jumpin' off is the surest way to be hurt - or to kill yerself. Ye heard me: kill yerself!" Why did he have to say that *twice*? Once was more than enough. I try not to pay attention to him anymore.

Two days later we rumble across a bridge. At the exact moment that he announces, "That be the Poulson Bridge over the River Tamar, we be in Cornwall now!" our coach throws a wheel. I scream as loudly as everybody else as I slide off my seat. Confusion reigns, but nobody is hurt and I am mortified when, instead of attacking, the 'villain' helps me to my feet and the 'murderer' offers me a scented handkerchief. So much for seeing danger where there is none and laboring under the silly assumption that everything that happens has to do with me - it does not! We stand around, converse as repairs are made and I smile for the first time since I left London. When we continue I let myself look out of the small window although there is not much to see except that the country is getting wilder-looking and more sparsely populated.

We are traveling on a post road, the helpful squire keeps instructing us. He points out the toll houses with their oddly angled front walls: they have large windows which allow a sitting guard to keep the road under observation in both directions without having to bestir himself. "Nobody but nobody gets through without paying toll these days," he explains and I cannot help wondering - how does he know? Did he try?

My new confidence lasts until the following night when a noise wakes me out of a sound sleep in my room at the White Hart, the only Inn in a small village. A loose shutter banging against the wall may have been the culprit, but now I smell smoke and that is not possible. I extinguished my candle – I am very careful about snuffing out candles, I even wait for the waxy smell that lingers on in the room afterwards. I jump off the bed and run to the door. Frantically I pump the handle up and down until I remember, silly goose that I am, that I locked the door and put the key on my night table. I grope for it in the dark and in my haste sweep it off the table. What did I expect? Of course I have no idea where it landed and cannot waste time searching for it without a light. What now? Screaming for help behind a locked door makes no sense. Which leaves the window, if it can be opened wide ... it can, and the chilly night air clears my head. Earlier in the evening I had noticed that big old tree some of whose branches touch the wall and my window: that is the way out and down, the only one. It's like our old apricot tree at home, I tell myself, I have climbed that since I was six years old and I still do it every summer to get Olga the largest, juiciest apricots from the highest branches for her jam. Of course starting from the ground up and during the day when I can see what I am doing. Not at night and not wearing a cumbersome sleep gown!

But this is no time for dawdling deliberations! I knot the gown loosely at about knee height, get myself up on the window sill, steady myself by holding on to the shutters, stand up for a few seconds. There is a little moonlight, just enough of it. I throw myself at the closest large branch which looks sturdy. My hands smart, but they *and* the branch hold. I maneuver myself closer to the trunk and from there down to lower branches, getting good and scratched. At last I reach a branch from which I can drop to the ground. Fortunately I land on my feet and not squatting in the mud, but by now I must be the very picture of bedragglement if there is such a word. If not, there is one now! I undo the knot before I stumble around to the front of the Inn where I gratefully accept the lady-in-black's coat before my lack of proper attire makes me feel more embarrassed than I already am. I am relieved to see that rescue operations are under way; they include free dark ale for everybody in the Inn's tap room. My first sip is also my last one. We are told that the fire has been put under control and that everybody is accounted for. Word gets back to us a little later that the fire started with a candle dropped in the upper hallway by a guest who admits to having been 'a little 'tiddley' or 'more than half-seas-over' which is translated for me as meaning the worse for drink. He sobers up quickly, apologizes to sundry and all and promises to pay for damages. A spare key is found to unlock my door. My belongings are safe. Let that be a lesson to you, my girl, I continue the argument with myself: *not everything that happens has to do with you!* Being careful does not mean seeing trouble where there is none.

I remain at the Inn an extra day – in another room, needless to say - waiting for the transportation which has been arranged for me. Luckily the scratches I acquired climbing down from the tree are on my arms and legs and covered by my clothes.

I am now only two days' journey from Trelawney Manor and getting more and more apprehensive. What if Mr. Trelawney is not at home, what if there are other grandchildren, dozens of nieces and nephews, a host of other family members, what if he is surrounded by an immense family and has no interest in meeting another granddaughter? What if he is still so angry with his son for marrying without his blessing (if that is indeed what happened) that his anger extends to me, too? Face to face with him, what should I say? I try to prepare something although I suspect that whatever it is would fly right out my head when the time came ... please, dear God, let him be at home. I cannot have come all this way for nothing!

When the next coach ride deposits me in Mills Brook it is late afternoon and raining and no transportation to Trelawney Manor is available. I was prepared for that. Since there is no Inn, I do what I have been told every traveler in these parts does: I get myself a room above the country store. Mr. Penberthy, the taciturn owner, stares at me before he offers me a bed and two meals for one and sixpence, take it or leave it. I take it.

At supper that night I try to get his equally reserved wife to talk about the Trelawney family and ask whether she knows of someone who could take me there. She, too, stares at me before she says, "Aye, me boy Johnny. Mundys n' Thursdys he brings mail n' pervisions. Thursdy's tomorrow."

I ask about when tomorrow, but all I can get out of her is, "Bright n' early".

I doubt that presenting myself at Trelawney Manor bright and early is appropriate, but what other choice do

I have? I arrange to store most of my things with Mrs. Penberthy for the time being and go up to my room. It is still raining, and no matter how I huddle beneath the single coverlet, there is no comforting warmth and sleep doesn't find me for a long time.

In the morning, the rain continues, and I bless Sir Arthur's foresight in providing me with that hooded coat. I draw it tightly around me, open my umbrella and sit down next to Johnny. His open cart bumps down a rutted, muddy lane. Soon we are enveloped by a thickening cold mist which seems to be rolling in from our right.

"Is it always like this?" I ask, trying to break the silence.

"Aye." After several minutes he adds a three-word explanation, "T'is the sea."

"How far is it to the Manor?" I try again.

"Not fer."

I give up trying to have a conversation with him and go back to rehearsing what I might say and to wondering what it will be like, walking into my father's home. There are no sounds except the rumbling of the wheels, the clattering of the horse's hooves, and of course the drumming of the relentless rain. I am just about to wonder out loud whether this God-forsaken lane leads somewhere when Johnny makes such a sharp turn that it is a good thing I have been holding on for dear life already.

Two stone pillars mark the broader road we have entered. It is lined with yews and chestnut trees; their branches hang low with dripping rain. I try to peer ahead - nothing yet. It must be a good fifteen minutes before the outline of a many-gabled stone house emerges out of the mist. Realizing that Johnny intends to drive past the main entrance I ask him to stop, but he gestures to the rear where his deliveries are piled up under a tarp. I stand up and shout, "No, stop here!" Grumbling under his breath he stops the cart, barely giving me time to grab my satchel and to climb down before he clatters off again.

I run up the steps, past two scowling stone lions and into the shelter of the covered entrance and shake the rain from my coat. Silence surrounds me, except for the wind and the rain and my heartbeats. I pull myself together, use the heavy brass knocker twice and listen for footsteps.

Chapter X

After what seems like an eternity the heavy door creaks open. All the prepared phrases are gone from my mind when I confront the elderly man who wears some kind of uniform. Behind him I glimpse a dimly lit hall. An enormous tapestry hangs on one stone wall, ancient shields and fire arms on the other.

"I have come to see Mr. Trelawney," I say when I find my voice again, but it doesn't sound very much like my voice. Why didn't I make sure he was in residence? What do I do if he is but refuses to see me?

And indeed the man who I think must be the butler says, "Mr. Trelawney does no receive visitors at this hour," politely enough, but making clear by the emphasis he gives the words 'at this hour' that most callers are aware of this. Why didn't I listen to Sir Arthur?

"I know it is early," I admit, "but I had no other way of getting here - if I might wait?" During this short exchange the man has looked at me very intently. He looks undecided.

"Come with Johnny, have you? Well, do come in out of the rain," he finally says. He takes my coat and umbrella which are dripping rivulets on the stone floor and hands both to a maid who has silently appeared from somewhere. Signaling me to follow he walks ahead, through the hall, and opens a door into a large room. I walk over to the fireplace to warm my hands. Tall Chinese vases flank it and generations of gentlemen who I assume are Trelawney ancestors stare down at me from their portraits. I am aware that the butler's eyes are still are on me.

Seeing that I am shivering he orders the maid who had reappeared noiselessly to bring tea. He is still looking at me when he thinks himself unobserved and I wonder: is it because he has noticed the resemblance? What can I lose by asking?

"Did you know William John Trelawney?"

He nods, slowly at first, then in quick, affirmative little nods. His eyes never leave my face. "Aye, from the day the young master was born. Of course ... yes, that is ... " he says, but then his back stiffens. "As I mentioned earlier, Mr. Trelawney does not receive visitors at this hour. May I inquire as to the nature of your business?"

I have not come such a distance only to be turned away. How can I explain how important this is to me, that Mr. Trelawney may be the only family I have in this world, that all I want is the chance to speak to him, that I'll wait as long as necessary ... I am still deliberating how to explain myself when the door is flung open. I hear steps and someone calls out, "Stratton, did I hear the door just now?"

My ears must be playing tricks on me. *I know that voice.* I turn around and say, "Mr. Harwood?" to the gentleman's back. He whirls about, looking stunned but recovers quickly and is at my side in a few long strides, both arms stretched out in welcome.

"Miss Aglaia! What a marvelous, marvelous surprise! Words fail me ... this is so amazing ... so incredible ... why didn't you let us know you were coming? We would have sent a carriage for you."

I am speechless. What is *he* doing here, in this house? He had talked about many subjects on the coach ride we had shared after the failed hold-up, but not once had he mentioned Cornwall, or indeed a place other than London. How could I have let him know I was coming here? I have the queerest sensation of being removed from myself, of watching a scene which is happening to someone else.

He frowns. "If you don't greet me soon I shall think that you are not glad to see me ... and you are glad, at least a little glad, aren't you?"

Of course I am glad. More than a little glad!

Tea is brought in and served. Mr. Harwood dismisses Stratton with a curt, "That'll be all," and sits down opposite me. Slowly it registers on my confused mind that not only does he give orders in this house, they are obeyed - which means he must belong here! How is that possible?

Again he exclaims, "This is too marvelous for words!" He looks genuinely delighted. "I have never believed in predestination - fate, if you prefer - but finding you here so unexpectedly - I say, this is making a believer of me! It is! This must be fate!"

My head is swimming. I sit, warming my hands on the delicate tea cup and feel that I am being pulled into something I don't want to happen. I need to remember why I have come here, nothing else matters.

"Don't you see?" he continues earnestly. "Traveling in the same coach in France - well, of course that happened by chance, that was a coincidence, a very fortunate coincidence. Later in Calais – doesn't it look as if the entire world passes through Calais on the way to England? Even being on the same steamer is not surprising. But this? Meeting here, in such a remote part of Cornwall? That was meant to be, don't you see that? Don't you agree, Miss Aglaia?"

He persuasive and charming, but I have never believed in meant-to-be and fate, certainly not that fate arranges meetings between people! On the contrary, his mention of Calais unnerves me. That is where I saw him (maybe) talking to one of our hapless would-be robbers (again maybe). I cannot let him distract me.

Now he leans back in his chair and says, "Only one thing puzzles me: the reason which brings you here ... but never mind that now, I am so delighted to have found you again. Nothing else matters. You disappeared so suddenly from the Langham ..."

Of course he knows about the Langham, he had confirmed my reservation there, but how did he know that I moved to another hotel? Suddenly something much more important emerges out of my disjointed thoughts: he gives orders here, his orders are obeyed, he may make it possible to ...

"I came here to see Mr. Trelawney," I say quickly before I can change my mind.

"Not to discuss business matter, I take it," he laughs, "you are far too pretty and too young to bother your head with mining matters. That's what Trelawneys have done for ages, mining. Copper and tin mainly."

I dislike condescending comments about being too pretty and too young to understand something, but keeping in mind why I am here, I only say, "I have come to see Mr. Trelawney on a personal matter."

"I see. Of course that can be arranged. I had no idea you know Uncle."

Just when I think that this conversation couldn't possibly take a stranger turn, it does. "Mr. Trelawney is your ... uncle?"

"Well, not strictly speaking, but my brother and I have called him Uncle for years although our relationship is a more distant one. I had no idea you knew him."

"Well, I don't know him. Not yet, I mean. But I must see him."

"And see him you shall. I think just before luncheon might be a good time. Meanwhile I shall have Stratton show you to one of the guest rooms and have word sent to the boy to return with whatever you have left at the Penberthys." He rises, and taking my hand to his lips says, "Welcome, welcome to Trelawney Manor, Miss Aglaia. I give you fair warning: I am not about to lose sight of you again." He smiles again and is gone.

In a daze I follow Stratton upstairs. How did Mr. Harwood know that I had stayed overnight at the Penberthys? Because everybody does, I remind myself. Stratton throws open a door, makes sure everything is as it should be, and I quickly decide to ask him the question I hadn't had time to ask earlier.

"You said you knew William John Trelawney – do you think I resemble him?"

Obviously he has had time to prepare an answer. "That is not for me to say, Miss," he says formally. "Ring if you require anything. Luncheon is served at one." Noiselessly he closes the door behind him.

I know, I know - I should never have asked.

I look about the pretty room. Tonight I shall sleep in this canopied bed whose yellow silk coverlet matches the upholstered chaise lounge and the two chairs. There is a desk by the window, small floral paintings on the walls ... and I may be only hours away from meeting my grandfather! What will he say? Will he believe me, will he accept me as his granddaughter? When? This is my father's house ... why didn't they like my mother? ... Mr. Harwood doesn't only happen to be here, he *belongs* here ... I don't know what to think.

I walk over to the window. The rain, slowed to a slight drizzle earlier now has ceased and a capricious sun is breaking through the clouds. I can see terraced flower gardens which slope down toward large craggy rocks and, further out, the sparkling sea. There is such a rugged beauty to the setting of my father's home ...

I comb my hair – what else can I do? Stretch out on the chaise lounge and look through the reading material piled up on the small table next to it? There are old copies of "The Englishwoman's Domestic Magazine"; the subtitles suggest fashion, fiction, needlework and household hints, none of which hold much interest for me. The "Illustrated London News" copies are years out of date and I am not in the mood for Homer's Iliad or the Bible, not even for Jane Eyre at the bottom of the pile, in the same edition Father surprised me with on my fifteenth birthday! I still remember being captivated by the opening sentence, 'There was no possibility of taking a walk that day' and having to know why Jane thought that.

I had also wondered why an English book instead of an easier-to-read German or French one ... but some of the things which used to puzzle me are beginning to make a great deal of sense. Still, I feel too restless to read, even to sit ...

Having been given a room, am I expected to spend hours sitting in it, twiddling my thumbs?

Would it be improper to wander around a bit in this large and very quiet house? Surely not.

I think about it some more before I give myself permission.

Chapter XI

I tip-toe noiselessly down the hallway when the sound of violent coughing coming from one of the rooms on my left startles me. The coughing stops, then resumes and gains in intensity. Someone is choking – shouldn't I go in and see if I can help? For Heaven's sake - no, no, no! One does not rush uninvited into strange bedrooms!

What should I do? Father used to maintain that, depending on the circumstances, action *or* inaction might be called for, and that it could be difficult to decide whether one ought to intervene or not. Never attempt something you are not able or qualified to do, he always said, but if you think help *is* urgently needed, don't waste time. Go. See what you can do. Help if you can.

The coughing continues.

I remember to knock, open the door a crack and peer inside. The room is in semi-darkness, but I am able to see an old gentleman who is lying on his side, on an immense four-poster bed, hunched over into himself - as if in pain? I go in, grab two pillows off a settee and carefully push them under Mr. Trelawney's shoulder and head – there is not the slightest doubt in my mind that I am in my grandfather's room! I pour water from the carafe that stands on his bedside table and hold the glass while he takes a few sips. When he has enough, he pushes the glass and my hand away. He seems to be a little more comfortable. The cough subsides and he lies back, but still draws breath with some difficulty. Small wonder: the room is airless and suffocatingly hot, what with the roaring fire in the fireplace and all windows tightly shut. He needs air. I open the window farthest from the bed.

Immediately a raspy voice protests angrily, "What the Devil do you think you're doing? Close that immediately! You must be new!" He is taken with another fit of coughing, but it is shorter and less severe.

New? I smile as I approach the bed. "Yes, Sir, I am new, but I am not employed here."

"Then who the Devil are you and how *dare you touch anything in my room?*" he barks. "Close that window and get out! Send Stratton in!" At last he looks up. With a sudden intake of breath, eyes narrowing under bushy brows, he commands, "Come closer ... *who the Devil are you?*"

Slowly and clearly, with my heart hammering hard enough to burst out of my chest, I answer, "I am William John Trelawney's daughter. I am your granddaughter, Sir."

He stares at me as if trying to see into the very depths of me and also, I think, trying to intimidate me. I stand my ground, willing my knees to stop knocking against each other but shaking inside. I try to look as determined as he. I find no trace of W.J.T. in his face, except for his blue eyes.

At last he breaks the silence. "The Devil you say. Hogwash, utter hogwash!"

I am getting used to his invoking the Devil with every sentence, but did not expect ridicule. "I have proof," I offer, but he only stares at me, shows no emotion at all.

Then, emphasizing every word, he says loudly and very clearly, "That you look *somewhat* like ... like William ... means nothing. *Nothing at all, you hear?*" There is a long pause before he says, "But since you have invaded my room, help me sit up!"

At least he is not ordering me out. I assist him while he groans, cursing the damn gout, the damn catarrh and the damn stomach pains - may the Devil take the lot!

I don't know what to say or do and ask, "Would you like me to ring for someone, Sir?"

"No!" Impatiently, he shakes his head and keeps glaring at me. Time ticks by soundlessly until there is a knock at the door. Stratton enters and starts apologizing as soon as he sees me.

"Never mind, never mind. Come here, Stratton.

Closer, man - I am having myself quite a morning!" He chuckles and some of the tension drains from me at the unexpected sound. "Tell me, does this ... this person here - she remind you of anyone?"

Stratton, startled out of his customary attitude of deference, clears his throat. "Sir, I ... that is not for me to say, Sir."

"The Devil it isn't. It is if I ask you, *and I am asking.* Come, come, man ... out with it!"

"Well, Sir ... there seems to be a certain resemblance to ... to young Master William."

"Seems to be? Are you blind? Look again. The eyes are wrong of course, the Trelawneys always have blue eyes, but other than that - I'll be damned if it isn't ... by Jove, I have to get to the bottom of this!"

I almost sag against the bedpost in my relief. I'll I be given a chance to explain.

"Yes, of course, Sir," Stratton clears his throat again, "but now it is time to ..."

"Yes, yes." Mr. Trelawney turns to me. "We'll talk later. Come back, to my study. Twelve o'clock. Go now."

I nod and turn towards the door.

"Wait! What do they call you?"

"My name is Aglaia Andermatten".

"What was that? Ag.... what? Forget about the rest."

"Aglaia," I repeat.

"Aglaia? What kind of name is that?" he grumbles. "Odd, that's what it is, damned odd! Of course *she* wouldn't pick a good solid English name like Mary, Elizabeth, or Anne. Odd name like that, must have been *her* choice! Well, never mind that now. Go."

My grandfather. Without discussion, explanation or exchanges of proof I know that this arrogant, proud old man is my grandfather. The way he voice had caught when he said my father's name, and he did see the resemblance ... I can hardly blame him for being surprised and suspicious, anyone would be ... and I had better ready myself for our next confrontation, he has made clear that he does not expect to be convinced. Another thing he has made very clear is that he despises my mother. His 'must have been *her* choice' was filled with such anger, such disdain ... Why can't he even say her name?

I don't think I can sit still in my room and wait for noon.

I go downstairs and find my way outside, walk along the terrace and take a path that leads through large rhododendron and rose gardens, still wet from the early morning rain, towards the rocks I had seen from my window. What awesome formations they are, rearing up straight out of the ground, forming steep cliffs going down to the sea. Far below, icy pale water crashes over submerged rocks. Even with the sun warm on my back I am aware of the violence of the sea, and for a fleeting moment the splendid isolation of this beautiful spot seems almost menacing. What a silly, fanciful thought!

I follow the footpath until it ends near some large boulders, close to the edge. I bend forwards, very cautiously - looking down is dizzying. I can see all the way down to the bottom where sandy pools, sheltered from the waves, reflect the sunlight. Seagulls and small black birds perch on the few stunted trees that grow out of the rocks.

I sit down on a nearly dry stone slab, hug my knees to me. What a strangely beautiful place this is, so different from our mountains and meadows, and yet so appealing. And so isolated. I wish Simon could see it ... and why on earth I am thinking of him after I had promised myself not to let him stray into my thoughts again? Especially now that the much more interesting Mr. Harwood happens to live here ...

"Penny for your thoughts!"

Startled, I turn around and look up into his smiling face.

"I've been looking all over for you, thought you might have gone exploring once the sun came out," he says and pulls me to my feet. I stumble, and quickly he catches and releases me again. "Careful, careful - especially here, so near the cliffs. This, by the way, is one of the prettiest coves on our coast - less dangerous, too, because it is not as rocky down below as the others, but there is only one way up or down, quite a ways south of here. Anyway, always watch your step, walking near here. Now how about those thoughts? I am still waiting to hear what they are ..."

"Oh, I was just thinking how beautiful a place this is."

"Beautiful? I would have expected you to say too quiet, or too lonely."

"It is quiet in my mountains, too. I don't mind quiet."

"Not now, perhaps, but what when you are housebound in winter? With ice storms beating against the windows, tree branches breaking under the weight of snow and ice, the nearest neighbors more than an hour's difficult drive away *if* the road is open, or if they haven't already left for the season? You might feel differently then - but never mind that now. I understand you are to see Uncle again at noon. Have you been told that he sets great store by punctuality?"

"No, but you are telling me now."

He laughs at that, and the walk back to the house is all too short, in spite of my impatience to see my grandfather again.

Stratton shows me into Grandfather's study on the stroke of twelve.

He bears little resemblance to the man I had seen earlier. Now he looks every inch the country gentleman, groomed, well-dressed, proud owner of all he surveys. Ensconced in an enormous wing chair, he disappears and reappears behind great puffs of smoke. His right leg looks swollen and is propped up on a cushioned stool.

"Don't mind this," he says, waving his pipe in the air. "Won't give it up, no matter what the learned doctors say. Not my port, either." He leans back, and even though I am standing and therefore looking down towards him he manages to make me feel that *he* is looking down on *me*. 'Try all you want, you won't convince me!' is written all over his face.

I don't know whether I should let him speak first or start explaining, but he betrays his own impatience by asking, "So - where are the documents that support your claim?"

"I don't have documents, but ..."

"No documents?" he mocks me. "Then what the Devil *do* you have? You don't expect me to believe you on the strength of a little dimple and the curls in your hair? Horsefeathers, stuff and nonsense! Well, what the Devil *do* you have? Speak up!"

I am standing in front of him, trying to steel myself against his bullying tone, his ridicule, his contempt – if this is the turn the conversation is going to take, what can I lose? I take a deep breath and say, "I would like to sit, Sir."

His eyebrows shoot up. With his pipe he indicates a chair that faces his. I sit down, scared but determined to have my say.

"I don't have documents or other papers," I begin before he can ask anything else. "They were either destroyed or lost in the accident." Much to my relief my voice is not very unsteady.

"What accident?" he barks. I don't know whether he truly does not know, or whether he is testing me.

"My parents died in the winter of 1847 when their coach overturned in the mountains, off the Simplon Road."

"Where the Devil is that?"

"In the Valais, a canton in Switzerland. The Simplon Road is a mountain pass that leads from Switzerland into Italy. It is actually an old Roman road." I know I am saying too much because I am trying to hide how nervous I am.

"Never mind that geography and history," he dismisses my answer. He seems to sink into himself. I have not thought of this before, but wonder - could he have kept a small hope alive all these years that his son might still be alive, somewhere, and unknowingly, I have extinguished that hope? He regains control so quickly that I decide I must have been wrong.

"They perished? What the Devil were they doing there ... you say they died, but *you, you* did not? That's not very likely, is it? How do you explain that - if you can?" He thumps the floor with his cane for emphasis and does not have to add that he doesn't believe me – his words have made that very clear.

"I am told I survived because I was wrapped in my mother's furs. She had also put this around my neck." I pull the locket out from under my blouse. "Help arrived too late for my parents, but the search party got to me just in time and ..."

"Where did you get that? Let me see it!" he commands, sitting up.

I slip the locket over my head and put it into his hand. He holds it up, brings it close to his eyes, peers at it intently and nods. His hands tremble.

"Where did you get that!" It is another command, not a question.

"It must have been my mother's. She must have put it on me - all I've been told is I wore it when I was found."

"The Devil you say! She had no right to this, this never ought to have been hers. Never!" he shouts, looking long and hard at me, then back at the locket.

I don't know what to say and think I had better wait for what he will ask next.

"Well," he says, calmer after a long silence and turning my locket over and over in his hands, "This has been in our family for a long time, for more than eight generations. It is always passed down to the oldest son's wife: my great-grandmother wore it, I remember my grandmother wearing it and my mother. Then my wife. Didn't know until much later that she had given it to William, to give to ... *her*. Together with a christening gown and other things she had bought *behind my back*. But this, I never intended this to go to *her! Never!*" he ends in a shout.

Surely he must know my mother's name; why can't he say it? I cannot guess what else is going through his mind and wait.

He pulls himself up and admits, grudgingly. "You see, this is the Trelawney locket. I suppose ... I suppose you might have come by it the way you say, didn't think I'd ever see it again ... it is back where it belongs, that is what matters. I'll let you wear it, for the time being. Here! But wear it so I can see it."

He watches me put the locket back on again – is he beginning to believe me? He must be, but before I can say anything, he fires another question at me. "Continue! What happened after 1849?"

I wonder whether he is deliberately trying to confuse me.

"You mean 1847, Sir." I tell him everything, holding back for the time being only that I also have the ring. His questions keep coming, one after the other, about the accident, why no one knew about this, who my Brig parents were, where I had learned English, how and why I had found out about him, why only so many years later – and most emphatically, what my intentions are, now that I am here?

I answer everything to the best of my ability except for the last question. "I don't know," I said, "I would like to stay here, for a while. I have no other family ..."

All at once I cannot say another word.

"And that's all you have?" he asks coldly. "It does not amount to much."

I nod. There is a long silence.

"Go now," he waves me away. "We shall continue this later."

I go back to my room. How naïve I have been. How could I think that one look at the locket would convince him? He needs more time. I have to understand that this is a shock for him. He did say that we would talk again ...

Chapter XII

When luncheon is announced, I make my excuses. I go over everything that has been said between us, weigh every word, every inflection. Then I sit by the window, worry and wait.

I am summoned back into his study at three o'clock.

Again he sits behind thick clouds of smoke, looking more unapproachable, more formidable even than earlier. "Let's go straight to the point," he announces. "All you have is the locket?"

I match him stare for stare. "No, Sir, I also have the ring."

His head jerks forward. "What did you say?"

"I said I have the ring."

"What the Devil are you waiting for - let me see it!"

"I didn't say I have it with me, Sir. It is in a London bank for safekeeping."

"And - what - the - Devil - is - it - doing - there?"
He hammers the question at me, cold eyes narrowing
with suspicion.

"My lawyer advised me to keep it there for safety."

"Ha, your lawyer!" He leans back. "Your counsel!
I was wondering when you would get around to mentioning him. Well, well, well ... *now* we are getting at the
truth! So that's how it is!"

I don't understand why he seems so oddly pleased
by his conclusion, as if he had expected this. I feel myself getting angry, only half-grasping what he seems to
be implying.

"What the Devil do you take me for, an old fool?" he
shouts suddenly. "What could be plainer? You have re-
tained counsel in order to get your greedy little hands on
this" - with his pipe he describes an arc that takes in the
room and everything in it - "because what you are after
is this: my house, my land, my mines, *my name* - the lot!
You might as well admit it!"

I have jumped to my feet at the first words of his ac-
cusation. Whatever is going to happen, even if it means
that there is never going to be a 'later' for us - I must tell
him how wrong he is!

"I have had *one* reason, one reason only to come
here," I answer in a voice that is too loud but shaky. "I
came here to find you, to find my family, to learn if I

had a family. I knew nothing about mines or that any of this existed" - I repeat his gesture - "and I don't want any of it! I don't need it and I don't want it! All I wanted ..." despite my efforts, my voice breaks. I know I cannot manage another word, and the one thing I will *not* do is weep in front of him. I turn and rush towards the door.

His "Wait!" is like thunder.

I stop, my hand on the door handle.

"Sit down!"

"No!" I am done being ordered about by this bad-tempered old man.

"Please. Sit."

After the barked commands his low 'please' touches something in me and I return to my seat.

"Come closer," he orders. His eyes bore into mine.

I am very uncomfortable but look back at him and wait - he will either find what he is looking for or he will not.

He hmmphs and clears his throat, hmmphs again, starts and stops speaking; clearly he has trouble saying what he wants to say, and suddenly I know. Admitting doubts, maybe even admitting that he may have been wrong - that is not something he is in the habit of doing. We stare at each other, and I know what he wants to say but cannot - I also know that he would have no trouble finding the words with which to dismiss me from his life, to throw me out!

Somewhere a clock chimes loudly into the silence.

I gather all my courage and say, "I *am* your grand-daughter, Sir."

He does not answer.

"I hope ... you are beginning to believe me?"

There is the slightest of nods, and under his breath he mutters something I don't understand, but it does not matter because he adds, "Stay. Please."

There are tears of relief and happiness in my eyes and perhaps a suspicious gleam in his? We rummage around for handkerchiefs. He makes a great show of blowing his nose. I wipe my eyes.

And then we smile uncertainly at each other.

Chapter XIII

From that day on Grandfather expects me in his study every morning 'so we can get to know one another'.

This being the first such meeting I am bursting with questions, and when he says, "Ask away," I do not need to be told again. I begin by wondering whether my father has or had any brothers or sisters. Do I have cousins?

"No cousins, no ..." A shadow passes over his face and I sense how difficult this is going to be for him.

"We had two sons, 'the requisite heir and a spare', like the old saying has it," he continues. "William and Percy. Good boys, smart, handsome, too. Both gone. First William, then Percy only three years later. Mary - she never recovered."

The pain is still there, in his eyes. Mary must be my grandmother. I don't dare intrude into the silence.

Long minutes later he sighs. "Might as well tell you, or - do you know already?" He sits up straighter. "No?

Well, William married against my wishes. That's it in a nutshell, that is what caused all the trouble. Never thought he would go through with it. How could he choose *her* over family, over tradition, over everything we Trelawneys stand for? I did not believe he would, not till the very end. There was a terrible row because I refused to receive *her* ... we said awful things to one another, never spoke again. Well, he made his choice!"

Grandfather's voice, dry and devoid of emotion, had again filled with intense dislike on 'her'. He blames my mother for the loss of his son and hates her, but I don't understand why.

"Who was my mother?" I ask, from a new sense that someone has to speak for her but immediately think I could not have chosen a worse moment.

His "A nobody!" is an angry shout; he dismisses her with a wave of his hand. "A nobody," he repeats. "William could have married anyone, including the only daughter of one of Cornwall' wealthiest families, but no, he had his heart set on *her*. Would not listen to reason, refused to see how wrong she was for him. Pretty enough, I'm told, not that I would know, I never saw *her*. She was not one of us, not from the right sort of family, lacked the proper background. Unsuitable, as I said before. She was a nobody. Sorry!" he adds in an afterthought.

How can he talk about her to *me*, her daughter, in such awful, hurting, demeaning words? I have to answer him, I have to. He will not like what I am about to say, but that is not what is important.

"My father loved and married her: that alone means she was not a nobody! She couldn't have been! He must have known that she was a good and kind person - and that is more important than the right sort of family which is right only because they have all the money in the land, or in the world, or because theirs is the most perfect, most proper background! And why bother to say 'sorry' when we both know that you are not!" It is what I feel and believe, but keeping that last sentence to myself would have been so much wiser. I may have ruined everything. Oddly enough, I don't regret having said it.

He frowns and looks daggers at me, but only for a moment, then he leans back, astonished. "By Jove," he exclaims after a while, and to my immense relief there is neither anger nor resentment in his voice, only a sort of amused bewilderment. "It's been years, *years* since anyone dared speak to me like that! Not since my Mary ... well, she used to tell me what a stubborn opinionated fool I was, she never minced her words!" There is a long pause before he adds, "Darn it, girl, if I don't see something of her in you!"

He chuckles while I sit on the edge of my chair, relieved but unsure whether to wait or go. I see nothing amusing in what I have said, and there is one more question I believe I deserve to have answered. Very politely

I ask, "Could you at least please tell me my mother's name, Sir?"

My question erases every trace of amusement from his face.

"No, I could and will not!" His answer is an angry shout. "I have forgotten it. And if, mind you, if - *if* I ever remembered it, it would not matter: I have sworn never to utter her name again, not as long as I live *and I will not!* So don't bother asking me again!"

I think someone had better change the subject, but I don't know how and there is another long pause.

Suddenly he says, "Where were we? William ... well, William left Cornwall with *her,* never came back. Percy was forbidden to, of course, but he saw them in London, a few times. He told his mother they intended to leave for the Continent as soon as the child was old enough to travel. Did I mention that Mary bought a christening gown and other things behind my back? I think I did. She knew it was a girl and wanted to go to London to see them. I forbade her to go: William had made up his mind; I had made up mine! I never saw him again." His fist slams down on the arm of his chair. I cannot imagine anything sadder than the empty defiance of his gesture.

"And Percy?" I ask after a long silence.

"Died in a hunting accident. Not even three years later. Mary ... she said she forgave me for not letting her see William and the child. She said the words, but I was never sure ... and she was never the same after we lost Percy, too. She died later that year."

What could I say? Losing both sons and his wife within such a short time, so many years spent in grief and loneliness, perhaps with regrets? No, perhaps not regrets. I doubt it is in him to blame himself, but there is a deep sadness in him ... I reach out and try to take his hand, but he pulls his away.

After another long silence he asks whether I would let Rupert bring the ring down from London on his next visit.

"Rupert?"

"Geoffrey's brother, I forgot you haven't met. The boys are only distantly related to me, cousins of cousins of cousins on their mother's side, that sort of thing. A lesser branch of the family. At present Rupert is in London, I'd like him to bring the ring home – if you have no objections."

Why would I have objections? I am happy to agree.

"It will remain yours, *for the time being*," he adds, and when, all of a sudden, he says, "now let's leave the past behind and talk about the present and the future," he becomes someone who has many important plans for that future to discuss. It has really happened. He believes me. He wouldn't say that I should go on wearing the locket and that the ring belongs to me if he didn't. He needs that 'for the time being' for his stubborn pride which, I am beginning to understand, is a very large part of his nature.

I sit quietly, overcome with many emotions and rather incredulous while he thinks out loud: teas with the neighbors, outfitting me properly, having my portrait painted (wearing the locket, of course!), perhaps a London season (whatever that is), having Mrs. Teague introduce me to running the house (a terrifying prospect). The list goes on and on, but all I hear in everything is that he wants everybody to know that I am his granddaughter.

My belongings are moved to a larger, more luxurious room, and for the first time in my life I don't do my own unpacking – Maisie is to be my maid, she says and will take care of everything for me. She seems very young and shy; when I ask her age, she blushingly admits to "closin' in on thirteen, Miss, but I learnt from me sister who was a lady's maid 'fore she was wed. I learn quick."

Grandfather and I dine together that evening, without Geoffrey who had to leave on mining business. Slowly, the reality of my new life anchors itself within me: I am really sitting at this long table which gleams with crystal and silver, across from my grandfather who raises his glass to me and with an immensely satisfied smile pronounces, "Pysk, Cober ha Sten, Aglaia!"

I can tell how greatly he enjoys my bewildered look when I ask, "*What* are we drinking to, Sir?"

"Fish, copper and tin, of course! Time you learned our traditional Cornish toast, granddaughter. The three have been part of Cornwall history and life for centuries, and that includes generations and generations of Trelawneys!"

Suddenly serious, he quietly adds, "I look at you and see ... "

Later that evening, too excited and exhausted to fall asleep, I write half a dozen long letters and include a short one to JustBen in Sir Arthur's letter. I am wondering how he is adapting to living a more regular life and how he is getting on in school. Sir Arthur, of course, receives a detailed account of how I found my grandfather. I would have given anything for heart-to-heart talks with Monique and Olga, and to be able to talk with Uncle Kaspar and ... and with Simon, too ... here he is again, intruding where I don't want him to go. He is not answering my letters – when will I grasp the fact that I am gone from his mind? I am not going to let myself get weepy over him ever again! How much better to think about Geoffrey who is expected back within a week.

I do and fall asleep very quickly.

The next few days are beautiful summer days, and time passes in a flurry of activities.

I meet the entire staff (which is not very large) and find that Mrs. Teague, the housekeeper, is a warm-hearted woman who tempers her iron-fisted rule of the Trelawney household with humor. We like each other immediately. At Grandfather's request she guides me through her domain which includes the spacious kitchen where the cook, Mrs. Chillicott, demonstrates her pride and joy, the new oven which has separate compartments for a steam closet, pastry oven, fast oven, bath boiler, hot closet and goodness what else. Then she points out the new airing cupboards positioned next to the hot water pipes. I admire everything from a respectful distance. Of course everything is much larger and more elaborate than what I am used to.

When I come up from this tour of inspection, from cellars to the attic, my head whirling with undigested information, Stratton tells me that I am expected at the stables, without delay, if possible. He points me in the right direction. Off I go to the stables where Grandfather is waiting for me.

"Ah, there you are!" he exclaims. He waits until I have come close enough to touch the beautiful chestnut horse whose reins he is holding. "He is yours," he says casually. "You do ride, don't you? Never thought to ask. If not, Geoffrey or Burton will teach you ..."

I nod, speechless, before I manage, "Yes, I do, I learned to ride when I was ten". Father had taught me the summer my mother died. "But never such a magnificent horse. This is ... truly ... this is much too generous a gift.

I cannot possibly ..."

" You cannot accept him? Stuff n' nonsense!" Grandfather enjoys how his surprise has me stammering. "You can and you shall. He is yours, and that's that!"

"What is his name?" I ask, stroking my present.

He shrugs. "Hm, never thought to ask. Well, he is *your* horse now, *you* name him!"

"But ..."

"No buts about it. Choose a name for him - and of course let Mrs. Teague know what you require in the way of riding habits, boots et cetera. Now think of a name for him, and that's that!"

I think for another moment and then I know! "Truly, I cannot thank you enough, Grandfather," I tell him. "I should like to call him That's That - if you approve." This pleases Grandfather so much that he chuckles about it for quite some time.

We are growing comfortable with each other and talk freely about many subjects, not at all about some others. When I tell him that I like to read, he says to help myself to anything in the library that interests me, and that there are books from which I could learn quite a bit about Cornwall history and customs.

He also has the music room unlocked, walks me over to a covered pianoforte and asks if I play.

"Yes - but only pieces which are not too difficult and not too fast."

That makes him laugh. "Easy and slow is fine with me, my dear. This ..." gently he touches the piano, "this was your grandmother's, it is a Webster & Horsfal, a fine instrument. No one has touched it since ... well, play whenever you like. Use her music, it's all in there." He points to the painted music cabinet on whose doors cherubs holding various instruments float among fluffy white clouds. I look around the pretty room, with the chaise lounge near a large window from which, he says, she used to love to look down to her rose and rhododendron gardens. Beethoven and Mozart busts stand guard on top of a book case; I don't recognize the other composers. I thank him, several times, until he says, "Enough, enough. It'll be good to hear the piano played again; of course wait until it has been tuned."

While we talk an idea is taking shape, settling itself firmly in my head. "Did she have a favorite piece, or is there something *you* especially liked?"

He nods. "All her music was sent down from Novello, the London music publisher," he explains and pauses for a moment. "Yes, there was something. 'Songs' - no, not only songs, it was songs and something else - songs - 'Songs without Words', that's it! She played those all the time. Cannot think of the composer's name, German chap who lived in London for a while, died very young, she told me ... well, everything is in the music cabinet. I haven't thought of this in a very long time ..."

Right then and there I decide to find the easiest and slowest 'Song without Words". I hope there is one in an easy key like C-major.

We speak about my father only rarely and never about my mother. I understand that there is too much pain in the past, that only the present and the future are important to him. I grow very fond of him in a very short time and sense that my presence means a great deal to him.

Last, but certainly not least, Geoffrey spends as much time with me as he possibly can. He tells me over and over again how he had kept hoping against hope that we would meet again, and how he will always thank Fate that we did. He is attentive, solicitous and looks at me in a way that makes me feel more cherished than I have ever thought possible.

The first time I ask him about his family his face closes and he steers the conversation towards another subject, saying he prefers not to revisit the past, ever. Sometime later he explains why - his childhood memories are un-happy, he says, 'worse than unhappy'. Naturally I want to know more. Scowling, he admits that he was afraid of his father, a bad-tempered man, usually absent but explod-ing into drunken rages whenever he came around; he dis-appeared for good when Rupert was nearly twelve and he eight. Their mother, always delicate, could not cope on her own and took her sons to her only family, a childless aunt and uncle. She died a few months later.

"You really want to hear the rest?"

"Of course I do."

"Well, feeling called upon to do their Christian duty by us, Auntie and Uncle dumped us in a boarding school the very next day *as charity pupils!* Do I have to draw you a picture?" he asks bitterly. "I thought not. Religion was rammed down our throats each and every day, but did we ever have enough to eat? Never! Rupert protected me from the older boys, bullies all. We ran away after a few years, actually before we could be expelled for one of Rupert's practical jokes which had gone too far this time," he half-smiles at the memory. "Don't ask about what we did then, the details are ugly; we did whatever it took to stay alive. All you need to know is that I would not have survived without my brother. Several years later Uncle tracked us down and here we are ... but please, let's not talk about this again."

I like Geoffrey a great deal and also feel pity for him, and every day my reservations about finding him here lessen. Why couldn't he be right - perhaps we were meant to meet again? Do all coincidences have to be cause for alarm? Why couldn't some be good, maybe even wonderful? After some months I realize that he cares deeply for me (apparently I am the last person in Trelawney

Manor to become aware of this) and I suspect I am falling in love – what else could this new feeling be?

And yet Simon still intrudes into my thoughts, as if he were somehow woven into my life. I keep asking myself: when am I going to face the fact that I don't matter to him?

Olga, of course, writes very often. In every letter she cautions me 'not to get carted away' and asks whether I really, truly know 'my head' (meaning my mind). I miss her caring, her loyalty, her no-nonsense approach to life, her way of speaking - even when she sprinkles it with those annoying Hungarian words. I don't even mind that she calls me 'Child' in every letter ...

Grandfather seems very pleased about the growing affection between his granddaughter and nephew. More than once I catch him looking at us, a speculative gleam in his eye ... it is not difficult to guess in what direction his thoughts are moving! Not that Geoffrey has said anything, and I am happy to have things as they are. So much had happened and changed within a short time that I am relieved not to have to make important decisions. Business has called him to London again; I need that time to think about everything ...

When we say good-bye he asks, ever the gentleman, whether he may kiss me. As if he needed permission. It is a very sweet kiss ...

During his absence I spend much of my time looking at the books and paintings in the library, a wonderful and inviting room, full of comfortable leather armchairs, ancient globes, maps, etchings and paintings, and hundreds of books shelved with no regard to any system whatsoever. I feel that I am on a treasure hunt every time I enter.

One engraving I find especially intriguing. It shows gigantic waves advancing towards and hitting the western Cornwall coast in 1775. Below the engraving is an excerpt from an eyewitness account which describes "these mighty hilles of water and waves that are affirmed to have runned with a swiftness so incredible as that no gray-houndes could have escaped by running before them." There is something endearingly quaint about measuring speed against gray hounds. Today, nearly one hundred years later, a comparison would probably be made against our fast trains. I find a book which explains that the eight-to-ten-foot waves were caused by the devastating earthquake which struck Lisbon, Portugal on All Saints Day an hour earlier and forget all about quaintness: within ten minutes the quake destroyed the city, leveled palaces and churches and government buildings. What was left standing was consumed by fires later that day. More than fifty thousand people are said to have lost their lives.

I think that doing some reading about Cornwall mining which seems to have a language all its own would please Grandfather. So I try to remember that kibbles are large iron buckets used to lift ore to the surface, winzes are smaller shafts, and girls (some only six years old) and women who work *outside* the mines are called 'bal maidens'. 'Holing into the house of water' refers to the extremely dangerous work in an *under-the-sea* mine, 'returning to grass' means to come back up from the mine, usually after a ten-hour workday and before the long walk home. There is much, much more.

I am curious when I reach two pages devoted to 'pasties', since centuries the traditional miners' food. A pasty is described as small, portable and filling. It consists of diced potatoes, onions, carrots, ground meat (if available) all of which are baked in a pastry shell with the edges crimped for easy holding, in other words a pot pie without the pot. It may be warmed by putting it on a shovel which in turn is held over a head-light candle and it is always eaten by hand. The article ends with 'Woe betide anyone who takes another person's pasty!' And according to an old Cornish superstition it is advisable to drop the last pasty corner on the ground - for the 'knockers', mine gremlins who will cause accidents, malfunctions and mine collapses if they are not fed regularly!

When I get to a section about mine accidents, I am dismayed at how long the list is: explosions, tunnel cave-ins, fires, floods, rock falls from roofs, equipment failures. There is also the constant exposure to arsenic dust which is produced during copper smelting and is responsible for poisoning and various eye and lung ailments. There remains much more to read, but what I have learned is enough to leave me with the troubling knowledge that my luxurious surroundings have been acquired at great cost. Of course there is an entire chapter devoted to the 'Mineral Lords', their vast estates and large ornamental gardens which shield them and their families from ever having to set eyes on where their wealth has come from.

On another day I am pulled into Cornwall's wrecking history - it is perhaps not so surprising that there is one, given Cornwall's rugged coastline. Apparently lights were set up to steer approaching vessels onto the rocks instead of to safety. As ships broke apart, local gangs would help themselves to the cargo and disappear into tunnels conveniently carved out between the coast and Inns and other suitable getaway places; some tunnels even ended in cemeteries under grave stones and slabs which had to be muscled aside to gain access to the loot - all of this while trying to evade the King's soldiers and excise men! Macabre in the case of cemeteries and of course highly illegal - but still flourishing and profitable at the turn of the century, the book claims.

When Geoffrey returns, he comes to me in the music room, carrying a bouquet of red roses, and before he says one word I know he is going to propose.

"I have your grandfather's permission to speak to you," he begins earnestly, holding his flowers out to me.

"I suppose ... I mean, you probably already know ... darn it, I've been practicing this for days and now the words are all gone from my mind. I'll have to start all over again ..."

"Yes?" I smile up at him. A tongue-tied Geoffrey is incredibly disarming.

"Miss Aglaia," he goes down on one knee, takes a deep breath and begins again. "Miss Aglaia - what am I saying? Of course I mean my dearest, dearest Aglaia ... will you ... could you ... will you do me the honor of becoming my wife?" The last words come out in a rush.

I put the roses down and go into his arms and we kiss. Again it is a very sweet kiss; I dislike the disloyalty of the thought which makes me wonder whether it shouldn't be more than merely sweet ... I cannot put a word to what I mean. We will be happy together, this is what I want for the rest of my life, I tell myself.

Grandfather is looking and feeling better these days. He loves to talk about his hopes for the Trelawney estate which, he never tires of telling me, has been in the family for so many generations. "But mining isn't what it used to be," he explains; "demand for tin and copper is falling off, and larger operations to the east are competing with us. Mines are opening in Australia, very large operations. Not only that, some of our most experienced miners are recruited away with promises of higher salaries in Mexico and South America. I turned the mine management over to Rupert and Geoffrey some years ago in the belief at the time that they were my only relations. Of course all of this is changed now. You are my rightful heir, one more reason why I am so pleased that you and Geoffrey will be married and living here."

Living here. Always. Was that a sudden pang of homesickness for everything I had left behind? I don't think so, it is part of knowing how I shall always miss Father, no matter where I live. I think about him, about the 'accident' and what might have caused it each day, even though thinking about it is as painful as ever. I don't believe that will ever change.

Of course I can live here. I know what it means to Grandfather, and Geoffrey's life and work is here. There is nothing that draws me back to Brig except my promise to Olga. And Barry ... perhaps both can come here, some day.

Sometime later Grandfather confides to me that Rupert is doing most of the real work. "Geoffrey is a dear boy," he says, "but he has neither Rupert's head for business nor his drive. By that I don't mean Geoffrey doesn't work hard, he does, but he needs someone to do the planning, tell him what to do, to direct him. Rupert makes all the decisions, of course after consulting with me. He can be ruthless, but that is the only way to accomplish your goals. Mining is a hard business."

I wonder why ruthlessness is indispensable, but soon push the question out of my mind. I know nothing about business except that around here women, young or old, are not supposed to take an interest in it. For the time being I am much more interested in getting to know the Trelawney property which I explore on horseback. I am also looking forward to the dinner Grandfather is going to give once Sir Arthur arrives in Cornwall. He is expected within the week and has offered to deliver the Trelawney ring in person. In his letter he explained, in typical lawyerly fashion, that he could not in good conscience entrust such a valuable and important heirloom to a stranger, family member or not. I can hardly wait to see him; I want him to see how well everything had worked out and how happy I am. I am also anxious for more news about how JustBen is getting on. He writes that he has grown a couple of inches, can read most anything and reminds me that that he likes to be called Benjamin now. I shall have to remember that. His last sentence mentions that he thinks he has spent enough time in school. Already?

I go riding every morning, weather permitting. Grandfather would prefer for me to ride with an escort, but by now I am familiar with my surroundings and he admits that I am a competent rider. He always cautions me to stay on the paths and especially to steer clear of engine house ruins (under which the copper and tin lodes have given out) because they sit on top of pits and caverns. I tell him that I do understand and that I will be careful. There are also abandoned and collapsed mine shafts everywhere, he also reminds me; they are treacherous because you only see them when it is too late - in other words when you are falling into one! He repeats his warnings about stray dogs. By law dogs must be muzzled when not penned up, but not everyone obeys the letter of the law and there is always the danger of coming up against a rabid dog.

I promise to be very careful and gallop off alone.

The morning of Sir Arthur's expected arrival is one of our rare sunny September days. I leave early, following the coastal path. I am happy and dreaming of all the happiness still to come when I realize that I have gone much farther than usual, to where the track splits. The one veering inland leads through bleak, slate-strewn and treeless hills which are sparsely covered by short grass. The land looks too stony for farming. There are chimneys and mine stacks in the distance and cottages. I decide to ride in that direction.

Nearing the cottages I notice that all are in disrepair - lopsided roofs, crumbling chimneys, rag-stuffed broken windows, sagging doors, rusted railings. Barefoot children in raggedy clothes play with sticks in the dusty earth; when they see me they run and hide behind two women who hang out wash on a sagging line. An old man who has only one arm – no, not at all old I notice as I come closer - sits on a bench, coughing and spitting dark phlegm to the side. Of course I had read about 'the miners' complaint, the 'black lungs', the wracking cough, the incurable breathing trouble miners call "bronkeetis" ... but reading about something and coming face to face with it, that is worlds apart!

Just a short while ago the sky had been so clear, so blue, but here it is grey and heavy with smoke that belches forth out of the mine stacks and settles over everything. Poverty is etched in every unsmiling face. No one responds to my greeting; women and children stare before they turn away.

Quickly, because I feel so ill at ease, I turn my pampered and well-fed horse around; when I think I am out of their sight I gallop back. I don't want to think about what I had just seen, but the disturbing sights won't let go of me. It isn't as if I had never seen poverty before. There are poor farmers in the Valais who live off whatever their patch of earth produces which often is barely enough for a family - be it wheat, flax, vegetables, fruit, sometimes vines. If they own goats or cows they earn money by selling cheese; if they raise sheep most of their clothes are likely to be homespun ... Father had seen to it that I was aware of how much easier my life was compared to that of other children. From them it is only a jump to think of the children *here*. This heavy greyness that hangs over the cottages here, that seems to cover everything with such hopelessness is different - the people here are connected to the Trelawneys.

When I get back, Stratton is directing the placing of flowers in the hall. By now I am well aware that he is an inexhaustible source of information on Trelawney and Cornish matters. I describe where I rode to and ask whether that was near a Trelawney mine.

"Aye, indeed, Miss Aglaia!" he answers. "That would be Wheal Lizzie, one of our smaller mines. Wheal Fortune is where the best Trelawney tin comes from, but that is to the northeast of here ..."

"Wheel - you don't mean wheel like this?" I describe an arc with my hand.

Stratton permits himself one of his rare smiles. "No, Miss Aglaia; wheal as in w-h-e-a-l. It means 'place of work' in Cornish."

"I see, thank you Stratton. The people I saw there, especially the children - I could see how thin they are and the cottages look like they are about to fall apart; there was a man with only one arm who had the most terrible cough ... do they all live ... in such conditions?"

He nods. "Aye, mining is a hard life, for both miners *and* families. Always has been. At least children under ten aren't allowed to work in the mines anymore nowadays, but accidents happen. A cousin of mine had a blast hole explode in his face; he lived, but what good is living if you're blind and a burden to your wife and there's three young 'uns at home? Poor man was already deaf in one ear, from the terrible loud noise down the mines.

And a friend's son was caught in a mine explosion: the hole went off, that's what it is called; everybody ran for their lives, but a stone flew out and hit him in the leg, tore out a ... well, he died from loss of blood that evening. Most miners don't live or work past forty; that's the way it is ... "

I had never heard him say so much and see that he, too, has realized this. "I beg your pardon, I have said far too much, Miss Aglaia," he says formally. "If you will excuse me?"

I have things to do, too, but what I have seen and heard today will not let go of me. It is time I took an interest in what has built Trelawney Manor and maintains it.

But not just yet. Not today.

Because later that day Maisie sets out my pressed rosebud dress and helps me into it. I have decided to wear my hair swept up for the evening and let her play and fuss with each little curl for what seems like ages. At last she hands me my gloves and, standing back, sighs and says, "Oh, Miss, if you don't look a princess, a real princess!"

I pirouette before the full-length mirror, smiling and not quite believing my reflection, and tell her that she has performed a miracle. She blushes with pleasure. Now even Simon's eyes would have to open and see that I am all grown up ... and what am I doing, thinking about him? It is *Geoffrey's* reaction I am waiting to see!

I float down the stairs, past the admiring glances of the staff, and into Grandfather's study. Grandfather beams his approval at me, and in Geoffrey's eyes I read everything I have ever hoped to see. He murmurs something that is for my ears only and I feel as if we were the only two people in the room.

I know I am finally meeting Rupert tonight ... I look around, see a gentleman getting up from his chair, putting down his newspaper and coming towards us.

"You are forgetting about me, brother, and I can see why - but please, *do* introduce me!" Rupert complains jokingly, but I am a little put off by the way he looks me over, from head to toe. We converse pleasantly enough although there is something about him I find vaguely disturbing. It has nothing to do with the fact that of the two brothers Geoffrey has been given all the good looks, actually looks like a Trelawney, while Rupert is dark and short; powerful, too. I don't know how to explain it, but I sense something cold and calculating about him which I think he tries to overcome or hide by being charming, too charming. I cannot shake off a slight unease being near him and hope it will disappear once we get to know each other better - I do so want to like Geoffrey's only brother.

Sir Arthur arrives, and after the sumptuous evening

meal I am more than ready to take him up on his sugges-
tion to go out for a breath of air while Grandfather sits in
this favorite chair and admires the Trelawney ring before
he secures it in his safe. I don't know if he will ever look
at the miniatures.

"I am so happy to see you," I tell Sir Arthur again.

"Thank you, so am I," he answers in his measured
way. "I can see that Cornwall agrees with you. I have
never seen you look so happy, nor, may I add, lovelier."

"Thank *you*. Yes, I am happy here, and it isn't only
Cornwall."

"So I gather, so I gather. Mr. Trelawney hinted at an
announcement later on this evening. I must say, I was
surprised at how quickly you decided, but I suppose you
know your mind - and your heart?"

Of course I do! I nod and ask about news of
Benjamin. He is doing quite well at school, but his
background, or perhaps his lack of one, poses somewhat of a problem. "He has been in a spot of trouble
with some of the older boys, but that is to be expected.
For the time being he has a much better life there than
he has ever had before, although he is of the opinion
that he has spent enough time sitting on a school bench!
By the way, you were right, he is a quick learner. His
great wish is to see your horse - you, too, of course! He
wants to know if there are other horses, how many, and
other animals."

Before we have a chance to discuss Benjamin further, Geoffrey comes looking for me. It is almost time for the announcement.

"You don't want to be late for that, sweetheart, do you?" he teases as he pulls me inside.

Not for anything in the world, I think happily.

Chapter XIV

Grandfather is already seated in his high-backed chair at the far end of the ballroom, waiting for us to take our places on either side of him. At his signal the musicians stop playing and what novels like to call hushed anticipation settles over the room.

"Dear friends, honored guests," he begins, his deep voice ringing clearly through the room, "I trust you will forgive an old man" - he silences murmurs of protest with a wave of his hand - "for not standing. As most of you know, I don't hold with long speeches. Tonight is no exception. You have all met and know my granddaughter Aglaia who has brought joy back into my life and Trelawney Manor. At this time I take great pleasure in asking you to join me in a toast on the occasion of her engagement to my nephew Geoffrey Harwood!" Champagne glassed are raised and drained, and before the musicians start playing again, Grandfather holds up his glass again, winks at me and mouths, 'Pysk, Cober ha Sten, Aglaia!'

I dance the first dance, a lively polka, with Geoffrey, then a slow waltz with Grandfather and another slow one with Sir Arthur. Because tradition demands it, I also dance with Rupert, but I am relieved when a neighbor's son comes to claim me. Rupert doesn't say or do anything I can find fault with, but I am not comfortable in his presence.

Geoffrey makes sure that from that point on every dance is his and I wish the evening could last forever. It is getting late when he takes me into his arms and murmurs, "Aglaia, my love, let's be married soon. Let's not wait! Let's elope!"

"Geoffrey!" I pull out of his embrace. "I could never do that to Grandfather. You know he has his heart set on a summer wedding, and I am only eighteen."

"Why wait an entire year? I think my mother was younger when she was married," he protests. "Summer next year - that is an eternity away!"

"A year is hardly an eternity - besides, don't we need the time to really get to know one another? You are away so much!"

"*I* don't need more time. I know all I need to know about you ... isn't it the same for you?"

"Well, yes, of course it is, but everything happened so quickly. I would like time to get used to it all, time to enjoy our engagement ... how about early summer?"

He pretends to think it. "Spring?"

"Please let's stay with Grandfather's wish: June or July?"

He looks disappointed, poor dear, but smiles and gives in. "Sweetheart, you are very difficult to say no to; I suppose I had better get used to that! Very well, but I give you fair warning: I shall try to change your mind every chance I get!"

Of course I write to Monique and all my other friends, and after some weeks congratulations begin to trickle in.

As I expected, Simon's first letter ever is the shortest. He sends best wishes, then goes on to inform me that Olga and Barry are all right, although Barry often waits at my bedroom door, whining and looking thoroughly miserable. Olga had to visit the dentist but is otherwise in good health. She misses me, has taken to arguing with some invisible person in loud Hungarian and clatters with her pots and pans more noisily than ever. That is the full extent of his letter! I reread it twice, but not even a hundred readings would make a difference. With a sadness I had not expected to feel I tear his impersonal communication into small pieces, because that's all it is, an impersonal communication. I throw the pieces into the fireplace and don't bother to watch them burn.

Uncle Kaspar sends his very best and expresses his satisfaction that Sir Arthur has been of assistance. He urges me to consult him if or whenever I encounter problems in the future. That makes me smile - what future problems, legal or of another nature, could I possibly have that would require his assistance? He will always remain a worrier, even now that Geoffrey is at my side and in my life.

I have saved Monique's letter for last, all three pages of it. This is what she writes:

My dearest, dearest Aglaia,

I read your letter a few times before I could believe it. So you are going to marry the handsome mysterious Englishman of your travels -- and your dreams! And he turns out to be a distant relation. It sounds like a fairy tale.

You ask whether I am ready to admit that I may have been wrong about my reservations. I must have been, you sound so happy, but some-times the number of 'coincidences' still bothers me. I know, I know, you'll tell me that I mull everything over hundreds of times and it's true, I tend to do that - but I keep thinking that your grandfather's estate must be considerable, what with a big house and property and several mines, so I still wonder: were Geoffrey and his brother in line to inherit before you arrived on the scene? Seems likely, doesn't it? How sure are you that there are no hard feelings? Please don't mind me asking this.

What is she implying? I love her dearly, but she is so

quick to think the worst of people; of course *she* calls it being realistic. I continue reading.

And now you had better read the rest sitting down. Prepare yourself for a shock: some truly bizarre things have been happening at school.

It turns out that Madame's cat, poor thing, was poisoned. Poisoned, can you believe it? No one knows why and by whom, but there is no doubt about how: the chocolate was poisoned, the cat lapped it up, the cat died.

And that isn't all. Madame went to pieces, no one knows whether it was losing Mr. Thornton or her cat, or perhaps both that did it. She was in such a state that she had to be taken to a sanatorium and she is still there. All the teachers have left and the school was closed, probably for good. Papa says schools cannot recover from such scandals.

The rest is chatty news. Linette now lives with them. They are both looking forward to my wedding and want to know what they should wear. She swears that she will not miss it for the world. Her letter ends

"Be happy, but also be careful.

I love you forever,

Monique."

I am dizzy. I had started to feel ill, with every bone in my body turning too limp to support me as soon as I read the words 'Madame's cat, poor thing, was poisoned,' but I had made myself read on.

Now I fall into the nearest chair and read the letter again. I understand what Monique writes, but at the same time my mind refuses to grasp what it means. I know, of course I know, and yet there is still that small hope that I misread something. Or maybe Monique made a mistake, or somebody else made a mistake ... I read the letter a third time.

Of course there is no mistake. I could read it a hundred times and it would remain the same. It cannot be clearer: the cat lapped up the poisoned chocolate. *The chocolate that was meant for me, the chocolate that two persons urged me to drink!* But perhaps poison that kills a cat would not be strong enough to do that to a person? What am I thinking: the chocolate was meant for *me*, not for the cat who got into it only by *accident!* Why meant for me? Because someone wanted me - what? Not only very ill, what good would that do? If not very ill, then what? Poisoned, *out of the way?* Yes, but why am being I such a coward, why am I hiding behind four words when one will do, the one I cannot get myself to think, to say - someone wanted me dead. There is no other explanation. Why? And what about *now,* nearly a year later - does he still, or do they still do? Who is he, who are they?

I pace back and forth, don't know what to think, terrible thoughts drift in and out of my mind, go off in so many directions all at once that I lose them. I must try to be calm, try to go back to the very beginning. Think, think: In Brig and in Geneva not one single person, not even I, knew that I was not Aglaia Andereggen - except Father, of course. You could have asked anyone and the answer would have been the same: 'Aglaia? Her father is the doctor; they live in Brig.'" Something else surfaces, only to slip away again ...

But all that is changed now ... changed because I am Aglaia Trelawney. Because. Changed for me, but changed to a far greater extent for Grandfather, for Geoffrey, for Rupert - especially for Rupert who makes all the decisions! And didn't Sir Arthur point out once that not everybody might be delighted to find out I exist - here is that elusive thought again; suddenly I know what it is: *Mr. Thornton and his clumsy attempts to get a good look at my locket!* Is it possible that *he* already knew, that he realized what the locket meant? How could he have known about its importance before *I* did? I don't know, I don't know ...

But ... he would have known if those two, Rupert and he, knew each other, now wouldn't that be a nice coincidence? Speaking of coincidences - how about my naïve eagerness to dismiss them as unimportant? And yet, I have been here for such a long time without anything happening, doesn't that mean that the danger is past, that there is no danger any longer? Of course it does, it must ...

I have given myself a terrible headache, letting thoughts and questions hammer at me over and over again. Rubbing my temples doesn't ease it, neither does a cold compress on my forehead when I stretch out on my bed and try to think, really think - but I cannot be calm and soon I pace back and forth again - who or what is there to hold on to?

Geoffrey, of course! Geoffrey has nothing to do with this! I am not being naïve about this, I know he loves me, I know he would never harm me. I know and believe that - I even believe that he lacks the calculating cleverness necessary to plan anything devious, never mind criminal. He is not due back for about a week. What do I do until he returns? What when he is back? What after that?

I think for a long time before the thought occurs to me - I could show him Monique's letter as soon as he gets back. Show it to him and watch for his reaction. That could give me the proof I need that he knows nothing of this. Immediately I am ashamed, needing proof, but I cannot think of anything else.

What do I do meanwhile? Go through the days keeping all of this to myself and holding on to the fact that nothing has happened here, the belief or hope that nothing will? Can I do that? I cannot burden Grandfather with this: one of his doctors is already concerned about his heart. He is still plagued with stomach pains, but not as severely as months ago, and at least the gout is not getting worse. "A lifetime of too much port, too much roast beef and too many other rich foods, dear girl," he often says with a guilty shrug.

I have to find something to occupy my days, to take my mind off this at least somewhat, at least some of the time! I cannot go on doing nothing but handing round cups at tea parties, keep practicing the 'Song without Words' I hope to master soon, reading and riding, choosing clothes, doing a little charity work and 'consulting' with Mrs. Teague on household matters - when we both know how smoothly, splendidly and seamlessly everything runs without me!

For the first time I give serious thought to how I spend my days and wonder whether I can lead this kind of life for the rest of my days. Wouldn't that turn into a life of ... of what? Comfortable boredom? The thought makes me feel ungrateful for all I have, but then I tell myself that once Geoffrey and I are married our lives will be fuller and richer. There will be children, our children ... and as if hit by a bolt I am reminded: yes, and what I have done for the miner children, their families? Nothing, absolutely nothing!

During the next hour I will myself to concentrate on what could be done and how, even though my scattered thoughts keep veering away towards poisoned chocolate, the failed hold-up, a smashed urn, my near-accident in London, even to the impertinent young man in Brig's booking office! I don't want to, but I have to see these 'coincidences' with new eyes, and when I do, I want to curl up on my bed and cry myself to sleep. I know I cannot do that: Grandfather would know immediately that something was wrong if he saw me with red eyes; he would not rest until he had extricated the reason out of me. And what good would that do except worry and excite him which would be bad for him, so I go back to thinking about miners' cottages!

When I feel I have something to suggest to Grandfather and the time approaches when I usually go to see him, I march into his study with an idea.

"Something on your mind, Aglaia?" He looks up and smiles. "You have that look ..."

"What look?" I ask innocently.

"The look that tells me you want to do something."

"You *are* getting to know me - could we talk about the mines?"

"Certainly, but these days they are more Rupert's domain than mine. Why don't you wait until the boys are back? Explaining mining operations is rather complicated."

"I'm sorry, I didn't mean operations. I meant the miners, the people."

"What about them?" I have his full attention now.

"Well, to start with - do they all live in those awful shacks?"

"Those awful shacks, as you call them, my dear - they are simple, I grant you, but there are roofs over their heads. Isn't that true?"

"Yes, except that from what I have seen many of them leak and broken windows have rags stuffed into them - it must be awful to live in such conditions, especially when the weather turns cold."

"Miners are a hardy lot, Aglaia, they have to be. And let me tell you something else: their lives are a darn sight better today than in my grandfather's time!"

"I don't doubt that, but the children I saw looked anything but hardy to me: they were skin and bones, some did not look healthy at all. Couldn't we at least have the worst roofs repaired before winter? Provide the families with some food and warm clothing?"

"The miners are responsible for the upkeep of their homes." He sounds as if he were reciting a contract clause; for all I know he is. "And that other - well, that is none of your or mine concern."

"Well, it should be!" That has slipped out all of its own; I know I don't have the right to say that. "With all due respect, Sir," I add belatedly.

Taken aback, Grandfather peers at me. "What is wrong, dear girl? You don't sound like yourself."

I apologize again and assure him that nothing is wrong, that I am well, but I also think 'that is the largest lie I have ever told!'

"Good, good. There is no need to concern yourself with these matters. And please don't ride that far again, especially not alone."

With that thinly disguised order he obviously considers the subject closed. I suppose that, having held the same rigid point of view all of his life he sees no reason to relinquish it. I had so hoped ...

He looks at me. My disappointment must have shown because he thinks for a few moments and says, more gently, "Well, perhaps, dear granddaughter ... let me think ... hm, as a matter of fact ... perhaps ... yes, as a good-will gesture in honor of your engagement, that *is* a good idea! So ... go ahead, have a basket or two delivered, can't think of what - well, whatever is suitable. But don't overdo!"

I hug and thank him and hug him again before I reach for the newspaper, but he says, "Not today, dear girl, I have to go over some papers."

I go to my room to start things moving by writing to Sir Arthur. I request the transfer of a considerable sum of money and include an explanation of what the funds will be used for. While I write I keep telling myself that nothing has happened since my arrival here, that I am not alone, that nothing will happen here, that I am safe here. At times I almost make myself believe it.

When Geoffrey comes back, I am happy and feel very disloyal as I watch him more closely than ever. His face lights up when he sees me, it always does, he is tender and loving and holds me in long embraces - this is what is real. He keeps an arm around me as he asks whether any important mail was delivered during his absence.

What luck - this is the kind of opening I had hoped for! I fetch Monique's letter and explain how I had been called to Madame's study and how she told me about Father's accident, how she and Mr. Thornton had urged me to drink the hot chocolate 'to calm myself.' How I left to go pack my things, returned to pick up Simon's letter from the floor and saw the cat lapping up chocolate from the broken cup. Then I say, "Now read this."

I sit down next to him and watch his face. It mirrors disbelief first, then all color drains from his face. He looks white. "Poisoned? The chocolate was poisoned? But that is ... monstrous, monstrous!" he shouts, getting to his feet. "Lord, when I think of what nearly happened to you, what could have happened! What if you had ..." Angrily, red-faced now, he paces back and forth. "They must be prosecuted, both of them ... how could *a woman* be a party to this? And Thornton, what the hell does Rupert still see in him? No wonder I never liked or trusted him, never!"

Not only had I never seen him so agitated, I have just been given a piece of the answer! Mr. Thornton and Rupert *do* know each other; that is important, even though I don't know yet why.

"Read the rest," I say. He does.

"Oh, my poor, poor girl!" he sits down again and kisses me. "How dreadful this has been for you." He puts his arms around me. I feel safe with him and so immeasurably relieved that I almost don't have the heart to tell that there is more.

He pushes away. "What are you saying? More?"

I nod, nestled against his shoulder again, but in a way that I can look up into his face. After tell him about the urn in Calais he can scarcely speak.

"But why ... why did you never tell me about this?" he asks.

"Because it was a windy day, after all that rain; I thought it was just an accident. It is only now, when I put this together with everything else ... well, now I wonder whether it was ... intentional?"

Geoffrey looks ill with worry. "You really believe there *is* a connection between that bloody, I beg your pardon, chocolate and the urn?"

"I don't know what to believe, but it's hard not to think there is some connection. Especially since there was another incident." I describe what nearly happened on Oxford Street but decide to tell him about Benjamin's part in it some other time.

"Dear God - did you see who pushed you?"

"No, but I'll never forget how hard the shove was, to the middle of my back."

Geoffrey keeps shaking his head, as if unable to take it all in. Then he sits, bent forward and head held in his hands. He looks worried, almost ill. He asks whether Grandfather knows about any of this.

"No. You know that his doctor is concerned about his heart. I thought he would worry too much and this might ..."

"Yes, I can imagine what worrying about you would do to him," he agrees, "but you should have told *me* sooner. Sweetheart, why didn't you?"

"At first I thought I was making too much of it. It is only now, after reading Monique's letter again and again, that I have become afraid, truly afraid ... but then I tell myself that all of this is in the past, that nothing has happened here, nothing at all ..."

"And nothing will!" Geoffrey interrupts me, shouting. "I'll see to that. You are safe here. I promise: you are safe. But you must tell me if something worries you, always talk to me - you are not alone here, Aglaia."

I wish I could believe that. "How can you promise that, when you are away so much? Aren't you leaving again soon?"

He puts his arms around me. "No, not for a while. Sweetheart, everything will be all right, I swear. My love will protect you."

That sounds so sweet and simple and so impossible, and yet he sounds strong and sure - how can I not believe him? I think of how he turned white, how all the color left his face when he read the paragraph about the poisoned chocolate. I don't know anything about actors and acting, but I doubt that even the most accomplished actors know how to make themselves turn *white* at will! Geoffrey has nothing to do with what happened; I know it, I'm sure of it. I am not alone. He will look out for me, he loves me. That is what matters.

After a while I ask him why he dislikes Mr. Thornton so much. He looks uncomfortable and will only say that Tony is a nasty unscrupulous sort who should never have been hired at any school, that he is a cheat and a liar and was Rupert's friend, but never his - and yes, of course he visited the Manor regularly some years ago, but the less said about him the better.

Mr. Thornton used to visit here reggularly ... of course he recognized my locket!

Chapter XV

Only a few days later I have a lovely surprise: another letter from Benjamin. It consists of five lines of fairly large letters which still lean against each other, but not as tipsily as in his first efforts. They tell me pretty much what Sir Arthur told me: "Dear Miss I learn well but am afeard mor school is not so good fer me I read well now and like numbers too how is yr horse I wish I can seem him do you have dogs too Miss you very much yr obedent servant Benjamin." There is a nice flourish to his signature. He has learned much in a short time - if nothing about periods and commas! I miss our reading sessions and wonder - what if he came here? He would be good company for me ... I deliberate about this for a few days before I go to Grandfather.

He does think for a few moments before he says, "Why not?" With a sly smile he adds that I had better not make a habit of picking up stray boys! He thinks that Benjamin might make himself useful around the stables since one of the grooms had to be let go just recently. "In time this may lead to a regular apprenticeship in caring for horses and equipment under Burton, *if* he takes to the work and does well."

"With pay?"

"How did I know you were going to ask that! First let's see how he does; don't forget he'll be getting full board. Now don't go and promise him a permanent job!" Grandfather warns, trying to sound stern and not succeeding very well.

I immediately write to Sir Arthur again to find out whether Benjamin might welcome a move to Cornwall - of course I am sure he will jump at the chance - and am reminded of the miners' children. I add a postscript that the requested funds are *urgently* needed.

They are sent by courier to the bank in Truro and it is only a matter of days before I can go to Mrs. Teague and Mrs. Chillicott with my idea. After some initial hesitation ("We don't rightly know, Miss Aglaia, this ain't never been done afore, never!") they prove to be good allies, perhaps because both have family members who either used to work in the mines or still do. They take care of the details, efficiently and quietly, as I had asked: blankets and pillows for the Wheal Lizzie cottages, weekly deliveries of milk and corn meal or flour, to be supplemented by sundries from the Trelawney kitchen for which there is no further need, but which have to be used before they turn. Really getting into the spirit of our undertaking Mrs. Teague suggests barley, as weekly staple and later for planting when the time is right, barley being the cheapest grain and the one that all miners are most familiar with. And perhaps some used shoes or boots around Christmas?

"And some simple toys," I add, fully aware that we're going far, far beyond Grandfather's 'one or two baskets'. I know he won't mind.

Naturally both women inquire, at the beginning of our meeting, whether Mr. Trelawney had agreed to cover the costs.

"No, I am using my own money."

"But he knows, Miss? He knows 'xactly what we be doin'?"

"He knows in principle."

"Principle, oh!" They nod knowingly at each other and then, suppressing smiles, at me: we do understand one another 'xactly. I am promised a full accounting before Mrs. Teague arranges for a nephew to take care of the deliveries.

Everything proceeds as planned, and I find a quiet sense of contentment from doing something I should have set in motion long ago. If the deliveries to Wheal Lizzie work out well, I hope I'll be able to expand the program.

I suppose that sometimes, when one thing goes well, another one falls apart, just to keep you on your toes.

These days it is the heightened tension between Geoffrey and Rupert that has me concerned. There are times when dislike fairly crackles between them, as if they were locked in some terrible struggle. I ask Geoffrey what else happened; he says it isn't anything new, only the old business disagreement, too complicated to explain. I have trouble believing that and don't like that he adds, "Nothing for you to worry about, sweetheart".

Disagreements between brothers who work together have probably existed since the beginning of time, but their open and constant animosity worries me. Again I ask Geoffrey and tell him I am sure I would understand if he explained it to me. Again he answers that it is only business, adding "nothing to bother your pretty head about." By now I dislike the 'pretty head excuse' even more heartily than I did the first time he used it. I let it go because insisting would have led to an argument between us and he already has enough of those with his brother. Once we are married I do intend to ask him never to use that excuse for subjects he does not want to talk about!

About three weeks later I see a truly frightening side of Rupert.

He storms into the music room where I am practicing my 'Song without Words', shouting, "Why are you interfering with my miners? Who gave you permission to play Lady Bountiful?" He coughs and stands threateningly over me.

Dumbfounded by his temper and rudeness I keep on playing and tell him that I am doing nothing of the sort.

"You have the nerve to say that to me?" he sneers. "Don't you know word will always get back to me? And stop tinkling those damn keys, will you? Everywhere I go I hear the same blather about the Angel Lady did this, she sent us that, God bless our Angel Lady. God, it is sickening. All you are 'delivering' are problems, more problems!"

"That is neither correct nor fair!" I protest. "These problems have existed for a long time and they still exist today. You of all people ought to know that!" Having come to the end of my piece, I get up and carefully close the piano.

"*You* dare lecture me on something you know nothing about?" He shouts so loudly that he is taken by another coughing fit. "There will be no further deliveries, is that clear? I forbid it. What's more, I also forbid you, understand this, *forbid you,* to squander money on people who are none of your concern." He coughs again.

"*You forbid me?* I spend my money any way I see fit!" I try to move away from his spittle-spraying cough.

He bars my way. "Not so fast, cousin! Your money?" His face distorts into a mask of spiteful anger. "*Your money?* It is not *your* money. Not yet, dear cousin, not yet! You hear?" The intensity of his antagonism frightens me.

"Oh, but it *is* my money!" I answer sweetly as I walk around and away from him. "I am using my own money, money I had *before* I came here. Before! Which means I am not accountable to you about how I spend it!" And then I cannot help myself and add, "*You hear?*"

One could call it comical, watching how my answer takes the wind out of his sails, but nothing about Rupert is ever comical. His rage evaporates as quickly as it erupted. His fists unclench and he visibly strains to regain his composure before he apologizes abjectly. He admits that he has been unforgivably rude, totally in the wrong. He assures me that the following is by no means an excuse, merely a weak attempt at an explanation: the many pressures at work, the traveling, battling such a severe cold and sleeping so poorly - this is to blame. He apologizes again and again for losing his temper. He asks me to please, please forgive him because if Geoffrey ever found out how badly he had behaved towards me ...

I cut short his groveling protestations of remorse by saying the incident is already forgotten (which it isn't, far from it!) and that nothing further need to be said about it before I walk towards the door. He follows me, apologizes again and pleads, "If you could see your way clear not to mention my inexcusable behavior ... "

"Neither Geoffrey nor Grandfather will hear about this from me," I say from the door. That unease I felt when we first met, that I still feel? It is amply justified: I have just come face to face with the real Rupert. I have I seen his temper, his meanness, and, more importantly, I have seen how much he dislikes me. No, how much he *hates* me. In the past he has been successful in hiding it from me, but now I know, and I certainly won't forget. I must remember never to underestimate him, to be on my guard where he is concerned.

Autumn that year is mild and lovely, but like the year before I miss the beautiful fall colors of home when the light-green needles of our larches turn a bright yellow before they fall off, the deep blue sky is reflected in the lakes, the air is brisk and pure, the silence broken only by the echoing sounds of an alphorn or the piercing high-pitched whistle of the marmots, our orange-brown squirrels rush to bury their hazelnut rations under the trees and the mountains glisten with the first snow. I had always taken for granted that Father and I would enjoy the changing of seasons together for many more years. Inevitably I think back to his 'accident' ...

Once again the brothers are away. By now I know that owning several mines means making the rounds of the different sites and keeping a watchful eye on managers, productivity and steadily recurring problems. Of course I miss Geoffrey. When I write that I miss him he writes back that he misses me more. When he is here we are happy. Rupert keeps his temper in check and his distance from me - I am grateful for both! He is cloyingly pleasant - there is no other way to describe it! I am outwardly friendly towards him, but remain wary, very wary.

Benjamin arrives, taller by a good two inches, and suddenly quite handsome. I teasingly compliment him on his well-groomed hair and he admits, blushing, that now he washes it when necessary, "but never three times like yer done, Miss!" He cannot stop talking about the sights he has seen on his way to Cornwall. In just a few days if becomes apparent that he has a gift for handling horses and that our head groom takes a liking to him. Almost instinctively he knows what to do the first time he gets up on a horse, and after two weeks he joins me on my morning rides. I enjoy his company; he has become a young friend. Soon he knows the countryside as if he had been born and raised in it. He gets along with the other grooms, and the other days I saw him looking at Maisie in a way that made her blush ...

Autumn comes to an end and suddenly winter is upon us and an unusually harsh winter it is, first bringing strong winds and chilly rains, later so much snow that I am reminded of home. I am glad that repairs have been made on many cottages and that blankets have been distributed. Grandfather, fully aware that I am 'overdoing with the baskets', not only smiles knowingly: we have become partners. "Your grandmother would have done the same thing - she would have loved you!" he tells me.

Most of our neighbors have long since left for London or warmer places. Geoffrey is away a good deal, too, and if I didn't have the deliveries to oversee and Benjamin to tutor and ride with these would have been dreary months indeed. Knowing that I go out in just about any weather, two warmer and heavier riding habits were ordered for me, and Benjamin now wears thick woolen socks and boots and owns two sweaters, raingear and heavy gloves. He is peacock-proud to become a salaried Trelawney employee come January 1.

In due time winter comes to an end, the way it always does, and after a cold and unsettling long spell of April rain, May beings back sunshine and flowers and the promise of a beautiful day for my June wedding (Geoffrey prevailed; Grandfather agreed). Geoffrey has been back for a few weeks. "No wonder our bride walks around with stars in her eyes," Grandfather likes to comment every chance he gets.

Sir Arthur, whom I had asked to look into my mother's background, confirms that he will be here for my big day. There is a damper in his letter: none of his inquiries have produced results so far. It saddens me that all I'll ever know of my mother is her initial 'T'.

The greatest disappointment, however, arrives in Monique's letter which, for reasons unknown, was first misdirected and then long delayed in the mail. The sudden death of Sylvie's grandmother means that Jean-Philppe's wedding has been postponed by two months - which brings it to *one day after mine!* At first two very devout great-aunts tried to have it postponed for an entire year, but this was voted against by other Chevalier family members. Monique writes that she tried everything, but the new date is the only date convenient for both large families. There is nothing she can do, she is broken-hearted, and so is Linette. Well, I am broken-hearted, too, only more so! I understand that she has to be at her brother's wedding, family comes first, but I am disappointed beyond words. I have new friends, daughters of our neighbors; they are nice, but I miss my old friend with whom I have shared years of fun and gossip and silliness and confidences.

Naturally, invitations have gone out to my Brig friends. Vreni has only recently enrolled in teachers' courses and works on the family farm in the summer. Renate is keeping house for her father and three brothers and helps out in the pharmacy while her mother recovers after an illness. Of my Geneva friends Veronica and Ingrid accepted immediately and with greatest pleasure, greatest pleasure underlined.

Not unexpectedly Uncle Kaspar's traveling days are over. He hopes that, since mine and Geoffrey's are just beginning, we will come and see him soon. Switzerland is becoming quite a tourist destination, he points out in a postscript. As proof he includes a newspaper article which describes the first two-week tour organized and led the previous summer through the Valais and Bernese Oberland by a gentleman named Thomas Cook.

Simon, true to form, has sent stilted regards - what else? - citing an uncommonly large workload. Did he really think I would believe that? It is exactly the kind of manufactured excuse I have come to expect of him. I don't know what still makes me think of him ...

That leaves Olga who, with her deep distrust of all things 'fangled' (she stubbornly skips the new-) has trouble entrusting herself to a coach - no power on earth could ever get her on a train, or one of the larger coaches, or - may Saint Jadwiga help her and God forbid! - on a steamer. She distrusts rivers and lakes, and I can imagine the terror the sight of the English Channel would throw into her. She apologizes for the silly fears she can do nothing about and asks for an especially detailed letter. Like all her correspondence she closes with 'Child, I pray each nights he good 'nough for you!'

Of course I feel unsettled much of the time with the unease that comes from not having answers to the questions which weigh on me. I keep thinking back to Father's accident and still cannot understand why the snow where he was found showed signs of having been trampled by people and horses. There are days when I accept the coincidences as belonging to the past, only to suspect evil doings a few days later. Something is not right, but I don't understand what it is. I have lived here, safely, for nearly two years - that must mean something, doesn't it?

On the other hand, Grandfather's enthusiasm and improved health are a pleasure to see. He has come through the severe winter better than I expected and has spent entire days closeted in his study with two lawyers, his banker and another gentleman. After they leave he asks to see me.

It is two weeks before the wedding; I fear he may have dreamed up yet another idea for the festivities which I feel are already too extravagant. I had tried to convince him that what I would like is a simple ceremony, followed by a festive candle-lit supper, but he had brushed that aside, saying, "Humor your old grandfather who wants to see his only granddaughter married as befits a Trelawney." He knows just how to get me to agree. What could I do but say yes?

"Well, it is done," he greets me. "Come, sit by me." He leans back in his chair and puffs contented smoke rings into the air. He looks eminently pleased with himself in particular and the world in general. "Don't you want to know what is done? Aren't you the least little bit curious?"

"You know I am always curious."

"Good, good. Now pay attention and do not interrupt."

"Aye, aye Sir." After only a few words I realize that this is not the time for levity.

"Aglaia, my dear, dear girl," he begins. "First item: The legal formalities required to sign over to you all my Trelawney holdings have been completed. They await your signature. It is my wedding gift to you ... no, remember I said no interruptions. It represents doing for you ... what I could ... not ..." He falls silent while I try to find the words to express my gratitude for his generosity. "You know what I am trying to say ... but cannot ... no, no thanks are necessary. Second item: As you are probably already aware of, Geoffrey has consented to the name change. The legal work on this, too, has been done. After your wedding he will be known as Geoffrey Trelawney. I hope that pleases you as much as it pleases me. All that remains to be done is your and his signature in front of two witnesses." Deep satisfaction shows on his face. "Now when I die, I die in peace, knowing that there will be Trelawneys here after me. No, no," he stops me again before I can say anything. "I have lived a long time, too long I used to think, but you ... you have given me the chance ... dash it all, girl, I intended to do this without getting maudlin like an old woman ... well, you know what I mean, Aglaia ... all I need is to know that you are happy."

I'll never be able to thank him enough. I kneel down at the side of his chair and put my arms around him.

His hand touches my head lightly - as if in a blessing, I think, and he says, "No thanks necessary, dear girl," quietly and very gently. I have never loved him more than at this moment.

And so one beautiful summer day follows another. Everything seems to bloom at once, everyone remarks how Grandmother Mary's rhododendrons have never been more magnificent. Grandfather tells me again how these specimens were collected in the Himalayas by hired plant hunters more than a hundred years ago, and that others were brought back by Trelawney men traveling in China, Burma and Assam - not the bushes and trees themselves obviously, but their seeds or seedlings. At the same time Grandmother Mary's rose garden is filling with the most spectacular blooms.

If Geoffrey seems a little absent-minded at times, I ascribe that to pre-wedding jitters, a natural enough state of mind which, I am told, can affect not only brides but some grooms as well - not that the latter are likely to admit to anything of the sort! He says that the old business problem remains unsolved as yet, and that lately he and Rupert are more at odds than ever, about everything, it seems. "You see, I cannot forget how much I owe him," he tries to explain, looking sad, defeated. "For years he looked out for me in so many ways, fought for the two of us - being on different sides all the time now is very difficult for me. But don't let that worry you, sweetheart," he tries to reassure me and folds me into his arms.

"Wouldn't it help, wouldn't it be easier for you, if I knew more?"

"No, I don't think so. Not now, anyway. Perhaps some time in the future ..."

I don't want to press him on his because I am more concerned about why Rupert has not reacted to the changes regarding the Trelawney holdings and Geoffrey's name change. Of course he knows: nothing happens in and around Trelawney Manor without his knowledge. I believe that sometimes he knows things before they happen! I keep remembering how he screamed at me in the music room, so completely out of control – he must be furious about the changes, and yet he has not said one word about it. Why not?

On the other hand I have made peace with Monique not being here. I had to. She is still so unhappy about the date change that I wrote to her we would make up for it very soon. Geoffrey, trying his best to console me, had immediately suggested that we travel to the Continent on our nuptial journey - a term I had never heard before and dislike, it sounds so stilted. He promises that we can take as much time in Paris as I like visiting with Monique before we go on to Brig and have ourselves our very own Cook's tour. He looks forward to meeting my Brig friends and seeing where I grew up.

I manage, most of the time, to consign the poisoned chocolate, everything it means and all the other 'coincidences' to the back of my mind - certainly not out of it! I could never do that, but at least I don't think about this every minute of every day. Nothing has happened in nearly two years. That is long time, I tell myself.

I have so much to be happy and grateful for that sometimes I ask myself 'what did I ever do to deserve so much?'

I was to ask myself that question many times in the days to come, but by then 'so much' had taken on an entirely different meaning.

Chapter XVI

Three days before my wedding ...

Again I am awake very early after having slept poorly. I am thinking of my parents, all of them, and of Monique not being with me on this important day, and about what could have the brothers so on edge. I hadn't thought that the tension between them could grow worse, but it has. I am hoping ... I cannot even put into words what exactly I am hoping for. Perhaps simply being safe and happy once I am Geoffrey's wife ...

Instead of having my morning tea I walk across the cobbled courtyard to the stables. I had been told the day before that the stable boys, after finishing their first chores, would be working elsewhere and that Benjamin would be out on an errand for Burton, which means that saddling my horse is up to me. Father had shown me how as soon as I was tall and strong enough to throw a saddle on a horse's back.

I am getting ready to lead ThatsThat out of his stall

which happens to be the last one in a long row when I notice that I have dropped my gloves. I bend down to pick them up and at that very moment hear muffled voices coming from outside - Geoffrey's and Rupert's. About to call out 'good morning' to them something about the secretive way in which they speak stops me. I remain crouched down out of sight, feeling very, very silly.

Rupert speaks first, in a fast whisper. "You're sure we're alone?"

"Yes!"

"You made sure?"

"I *said* yes!" Geoffrey sounds angry.

"All right, all right. You know what to do?"

"Yes, no need to go over it again."

"Telling you once is never enough!" Rupert hisses back. "I saw the papers: *everything* is signed over to your bride. Meaning: no more pills for the old man; he'll depart on his own soon enough. You are to continue as the devoted lover until the signal - the one that'll tell you to switch over to heartbroken widower. Got all of that?" he ends with a nasty chuckle.

I try to swallow down the sudden panic that sets my heart racing and turns my hands clammy. I can hardly breathe, there is such a queasy feeling in my stomach that I press both fists against my mouth: I cannot be sick, I cannot make the smallest of sounds, I have to be quiet, very still. Geoffrey the devoted lover switching to heart-broken widower? Did I hear that, did I hear right? I did, yes, I did! Don't make a sound.

"*You cannot do this*, I've told you a thousand times!" Geoffrey shouts. "I love her! There's no need for that other, not with everything mine once we are married."

I bite down hard into my fist.

"Don't you mean *ours, brother? Ours!* Quit being such a bloody fool about what you so delicately call 'that other' - how safe do you think we we'll be when she finds out people have *died* for this, huh? Didn't think of that, did you, brother? We stay with our plan!"

"*Your plan, not mine!* I am sick to death finding out about 'your plans' only afterwards, when it is too late! I would never have let you ..." Again Geoffrey's voice has risen in anger and furiously Rupert interrupts him.

"*Let me?* Who in bloody hell do you think you are? We are in this together!"

"We are not!"

Now there is silence, but I have not heard them walk away. I want to cover my ears so I cannot hear more. They must still be here. But if there is more, I *must* hear it. All of it. A pain different from anything I have ever felt claws at me.

"Rupert, I'm warning you! I won't have it!"

"Shut up! I've had enough of your mistakes!"

"*My mistakes?*" Geoffrey screams. "When it was *Tony* who botched everything in France and in London - and how about his hare-brained scheme up in the mountains that you finally, finally told me about last week, *only last week!* How dare you talk about *my* mistakes?"

Rupert and Mr. Thornton! They caused Father's accident, they caused his death! And Geoffrey knew, not earlier, but he has known for a week! The roaring noise in my ears prevents me from hearing what Geoffrey is saying, but Rupert cuts him off again.

"Shut up, you idiot! Get it through your head: it is the only way it becomes and remains *ours!* Of course, it you are tired of living, you too could be ...

"You wouldn't dare ..." The rest of Geoffrey's answer is lost in the shuffle of their boots as they walk away from the stables.

They have gone.

What am I going to do? I want to run away - no, I cannot leave, not yet, they might still be somewhere nearby, I must wait - yes, wait. For how long? Fragments of the brothers' conversation careen around in my head, with Rupert's sarcastic 'playing the heartbroken widower' colliding with Geoffrey's pathetic 'but I love her'. This is not love, this is betrayal! This is lies, one lie after another. A business disagreement? Lies, lies, nothing but lies!

Geoffrey knew and kept up the pretense of not knowing: he knew on the way to Paris, he knew about London, he knew when he went on and on about how a kind fate had brought us together again, he has known about Father for one entire week - and he knew all the other times, when he tried to talk me into an earlier wedding date, when he read Monique's letter, he knew every time he told me he loved me, he knew how Rupert's plan is supposed to end, he knew, he knew ...

I cannot finish my thoughts ... and dear Lord, the pills, what are they? What pills are they giving Grandfather? How could Geoffrey become part of this ... there are no words for what he allowed to happen, no matter how much he believes he owes his brother ...

Slowly I get up and lean against the stall until the dizziness passes.

That's That nuzzles my shoulder - he expects his ride.

I listen for sounds but don't hear anything. They are gone. I walk my horse out into the cool morning air, over to the mounting block and gallop out of the yard. As soon as the manor is behind me my control breaks and everything I held down bursts out of me. Driven by something outside of myself, I don't care that I don't see or know where I'm heading, I let ThatsThat go as fast and as far as he wants. If I could have escaped to the ends of the earth, I would have. How could I have been so naïve, so blind, so wrong about Geoffrey, know him so little? He has lied to me about everything - no, not everything. Not about loving me. I still believe that, but his 'I love you', the words I treasured, mean nothing now.

Anxiety and fear and sadness fill me, but there is anger, too, and it grows. No, not only anger - rage, a terrible rage. They caused Father's death. 'That stupid hare-brained scheme,' Geoffrey called it. I don't know what they did and how, and in a way that doesn't matter any longer: I know that Rupert was behind it. I know.

I have paid no attention to the path other than to notice that I have ridden far, all the way to where there is a path that leads down to the sea in sharp turns. My horse slows down. I have been here before a few times and know what he hopes for. When we reach the bottom I dismount and let him gallop and circle across the sand. He loves the freedom of doing that and I lose all sense of time until he trots back to me and nudges my shoulder. I pull the apple I always take along on my morning rides out of my pocket, check his hooves for pebbles and I lead him back up.

This is not over. It will never be over.

I cannot think only of myself, I must consider Grandfather. With the lucidity of hindsight I marvel at how cleverly I have been manipulated. So foolish, like putty in Geoffrey's hands, so ready to be loved - but that foolish girl doesn't exist anymore!

I have to pull myself together, ride back to the Manor as if nothing had happened, that's what I have to do. Grandfather and I will be safe until after the wedding. Rupert has not said that in so many words, but he did imply it. They don't know I overhead them - they must never suspect that I did. I can do that if I keep in mind what they have done to Father and what they plan to do to Grandfather and me, whatever it is. I can. If only I didn't have such trouble gathering and controlling my thoughts, they float around only to disappear before I can grab them.

And now something Sir Arthur had mentioned rears up in the midst of all the confusion: "I am telling you this in abbreviated form and simple terms, but it is important: be aware that under British Common Law a woman's property legally becomes her husband's. In other words: what you inherit becomes your husband's property upon marriage. A widow, however, may reclaim her property ..." Strange that this surfacdes now of all times - no, it is not strange to remember something that so completely fits the situation. What is strange is how perfectly it fits: what Grandfather gives me becomes Geoffrey's upon our marriage. What a wonderfully simple, convenient solution for the brothers! I am struck by the monumental irony of it all: Geoffrey will own Trelawney Manor and everything that goes with it simply by marrying me! Of course there is Rupert's need to get his half and the danger of silly Aglaia tumbling on to his schemes which means ...

I force myself to think about Geoffrey playing 'the heartbroken widower' and a new chill cuts off that thought: meanwhile, how do I convince everybody that I am a happy bride? I am safe until the wedding. *Only until the wedding* ... I repeat that to myself, again and again. Can I do it? Yes, I can, but knowing what Rupert is capable of, what can I do about afterwards?

Sir Arthur ... he is due to arrive in one or two days ... if I could find a way to speak to him in private ... I ride back slowly, knowing that I have to arrange that, but I cannot think ...

I hand That'sThat over to a stable boy. Then I carefully brush all the sand I can see off my boots and the hem of my riding habit.

The first test of my acting ability comes sooner than expected. Geoffrey and I literally bump into each other as I enter the house.

"Oh, there you are, sweetheart!" Geoffrey exclaims, "I have been searching everywhere for you. I didn't know you were going riding this morning." He looks at me and frowns. "I have never seen you so pale after a ride, and your eyes are red ... you aren't feeling ill, are you?"

"No, not at all! I had something in my eye, that's all ... I am really well, thank you, but still not sleeping well. If I had known you wanted to ride, I would have waited so we could go together."

"Don't worry about this morning, sweetheart, we have lifetime of riding together ahead of us, don't we?" He gives my arm one of his loving little squeezes.

We have a lifetime together? Really?

I force myself to say, "Yes, we do." I don't know what I should marvel at more - his hypocrisy or the ease with which I am lying. We walk into the Manor together. He puts his arm around me and I smile up at him.

I need to see Grandfather right away, before I change. I always spend one or two morning hours with him; adhering to our routine is important. I find him in his study, going over accounts with Rupert - no, not Rupert, I am not ready for him! I murmur an apology and quickly turn to leave.

"No, stay, my dear," Grandfather calls out to me, "We're just about done here, isn't that so, Rupert?"

"Yes, Sir, we are." Rupert gathers up papers and ledgers.

"You are doing fine work, my boy," Grandfather says. "Aglaia, your cousin, soon to be your brother-in-law, has a good head for business. He has become an excellent manager."

"I am sure he has," I agree politely. I keep my voice steady and force a smile on my face. All I can think of is that 'conniving schemer and ruthless murderer' would fit him so much better!

"You look lovely as always, Aglaia." Rupert's words are gallant but his eyes belie his words as they travel down and examine every inch of my boots and my riding habit.. "I see you've been out already. Long ride?"

What he means, of course, is 'were you anywhere near the stables when *we* were there, too?" Well, he is not going to trap me that easily!

"No, not long. I wish Geoffrey could have come with me."

Again he looks me over from head to toe, even walks around me and, I feel, gives special attention to my boots and the hem of my riding skirt. He doesn't even bother to disguise what he is doing, only smiles that insincere knowing smile of his. Looking pleased, he nods and leaves.

Grandfather and I are alone.

I pull the footstool over to him and sit down. "How are you today?" I ask.

"Very well. Never better. No complaints."

"What about your stomach pains?"

"Aglaia, what is this sudden interest in my health? Hm ... young ladies ought not to discuss such details, you know ... er ... details of that nature with their elders. Highly irregular, you know."

"I know nothing of the sort. Perhaps you forget that I grew up in a doctor's house. Grandfather - are you truly feeling better?"

"Of course I am." A delighted grin spreads over his face. He leans towards me and whispers, "Come closer, I might as well let you in on my secret: I have decided that the learned doctors don't know what the Devil they're doing most of the time; their quackery probably kills as often as it heals! So - after that last attack I said to myself: no more doctors, no more pills, no more potions! From now on why not let nature take her course? When my time is up - well, then it is up. Strangely enough I am feeling much better since then."

I don't know what to say, but fervently I think, 'Thank you, God, thank you!'

"By the way, there is nothing to worry about," he says, still just above a whisper. "I make believe that I still swallow their blasted pills, still drink those vile potions." He shudders. "Stratton helps me fool the doctors, the boys, too, and disposes of the lot. No one else knows, so not a word to anybody. Promise?"

My voice is shaky with relief when I promise.

"My dear girl, what is this I see? Tears? There is no reason to be concerned about me, no reason at all."

Gently he pats my cheek. "Aren't tears before the wedding supposed to be bad luck? Of course that is only a silly superstition, isn't it?"

"Of course, but superstition or not - no more tears!"

"That's the spirit!" He tries to sound unemotional but doesn't quite succeed. "Now run along and change, dear girl. I am sure there are many things a happy bride has to take care of only two days before her wedding!"

I kiss him and rush up to my room.

'There is no happy bride in this house' - how I would like to shout that from the Manor's rooftops so everyone could hear and would know! Isn't there *one* person who sees and knows Rupert for who he is? How could there be? I have been as blind as everyone else! Didn't I stumble only by chance on what he is planning, on who he is?

I must do something, but I still cannot think clearly. I *must* do better than this - there is only one thing I am sure of: I cannot do anything on my own. I cannot go to the police: even if I could get to the local constabulary (which is too far) without anyone knowing about it (which is unlikely), what would I tell them? That it started when my father was killed, that a cat was poisoned and died, that an urn narrowly missed falling on me, that I was pushed into heavy London traffic, and that they - person or persons unknown, except I do suspect my brother-in-law - are still out there, planning to get rid of me? It all sounds so ridiculous, like the ravings of an unhinged female who imagines fanciful dangers and attacks - who would believe me?

Perhaps I *am* becoming unhinged, at times I feel that I am.

No, help can only come with Sir Arthur! He is supposed to arrive tomorrow. Two days before the wedding. If I could speak to him as soon as he arrives - no, 'if' leaves too much to chance. Suddenly it comes to me, with a flicker of hope that my mind is beginning to function again: I shall send Benjamin to Mills Brook with a letter for Sir Arthur, to be handed to him and only to him, immediately upon his arrival. If Sir Arthur should be delayed for any reason, Benjamin will be prepared to remain there overnight. I shall tell him that my life depends on this! Sir Arthur will know what to do, I hope ... that is all I have, this hope.

A second thought occurs to me: in order not to arouse suspicions, I shall have Benjamin take one of my blouses to Mrs. Penberthy for repairs. I know how clever she is with needle and thread, I have used her services before. I pull a perfectly ironed blouse out of the wardrobe, crumple it up and tear the fine fabric at an armhole. I have never done anything like this before - but then I have never been caught in such an awful, terrible situation!

Benjamin, God bless him, asks no questions, but hangs on my every word as I explain the importance, secrecy and urgency of his errand. "I does anythin' fer ye,

Miss, ye know that," he says fervently. "It'll come out right wiv Sir Arther on our side," he adds, trying to console me.

For the first time since that awful moment in the stable I feel that all is not lost, that there is more fight in me than I expected.

More, I hope, than *they* expect.

Chapter XVII

I hold on to my belief that nothing will happen before the wedding, I have to, but no matter how hard I try, I cannot help being tense. Everything that Geoffrey and Rupert say takes on a hidden meaning. I turn their words and phrases, inflections and nuances in tone over and over in my mind until Geoffrey becomes aware of my preoccupation and teasingly inquires whether I am having second thoughts.

"Of course not," I protest quickly, "Only my last attack of bride's nerves before the big day, a small one, nothing to worry about. It happens to most of us girls, you know."

"So I have heard." He kisses me, but all that means to me now is that I must kiss him as if my heart was in it.

On the afternoon that Sir Arthur is expected, my anxiety grows so overwhelming that I don't know what to do with myself. I cannot read, I cannot sit still. Benjamin has left, dispatched on his errand hours earlier. He ought to be back with Sir Arthur before the evening meal - but what if they are not? I have already checked the drive several times and know I shouldn't do it again, but I go to the front door again and look down the drive.

"Looking for someone in particular, Cousin?"

Noiselessly, Rupert has come up behind me. Startled and trying for an unconcern I am far from feeling I tell him, very curtly, that I dislike people creeping up on me. "If you must know, I was wondering what is keeping Sir Arthur."

"Well, I don't know anything about his travel arrangements. Who knows - he may not get here until tomorrow," he says with that lazy, insolent smile of his. "What if he doesn't come at all? I wonder, would that be merely annoying to you or greatly disconcerting?"

"Why are you asking?" I can scarcely form the words. Did he ask that because he suspects or knows something? No, that cannot be!

"No reason, just curious why is it so important to have your *London counsel* present for the festivities."

"He is more than my counsel! He is a friend and - oh, never mind, I don't have to explain myself to you!"

"True, true ... but why so nervous, Cousin? There wouldn't be anything wrong between the lovebirds?"

"Of course not! Why would you think that?"

"Are you sure?"

"Of course I am sure!"

He moves closer and I take an involuntary step back.

"Aglaia, what is the matter? You are shaking like a leaf!" He comes closer still and I cannot bear being so near him, I back away again. Now something ugly and frightening passes across his face, fleeting yet also curiously triumphant. I think it is all over, he knows, he is toying with me ... he knows that I know ... but all he says, in perfect command and overly solicitous, is, "You are shivering, cousin. May I fetch a shawl for you?"

The urge to run away from him is overwhelming, but I manage, "No, thank you, I'll get one myself," before I turn and go back inside. He follows me inside and closes the heavy door. The sound echoes like a thousand doors closing on me. I am sure his eyes follow me until I am out of his sight. Did I give myself away? How? I have tried so hard not to ... and what has delayed Sir Arthur?

Sir Arthur has not arrived when we sit down to a late dinner which I expect to be torture and it is. Grandfather presides at the table. He is in high spirits and talks about the wedding and a wonderful future. A master at this as always, Rupert makes pleasant and clever conversation; Geoffrey looks adoringly at me and whispers sweet nothings into my ear. He loves me, I know that, I still don't doubt it - but what I felt for him has crumbled away into nothing. Everything between us was built on deceit and lies. Lies, nothing but lies. Doesn't he realize how he has betrayed me? How betrayed I feel? That nothing can be left, only incomprehension and a sad pity - and a growing anger at myself for having been so blind.

It doesn't take long for Geoffrey to notice that I am only toying with my food. He looks worried. "Is something wrong, sweetheart, are you still nervous?" he asks.

"Perhaps a little," I manage. My efforts are good enough to fool Grandfather and perhaps Geoffrey, but I am afraid they have not deceived Rupert. He exchanges glances with Geoffrey who gives a slight shrug. What does that mean? Is it a sign that he doesn't know, or a secret signal, or did it mean nothing at all? What if I am wrong, what if Grandfather and I are not safe *before* the wedding? No. No, I am not wrong about that: they need the wedding to take place!

A little later, full of loving concern, Geoffrey leans towards me. "Sweetheart, you haven't touched your dessert at all, and I know how much you enjoy Mrs. Chillicott's special creations ... how about some air? That might help you feel better; let's go for a stroll in the garden."

I pretend to give it some thought and say, "Not tonight, I think I'd like to go up soon, if you don't mind. I am tired."

"I know you're not sleeping well, and I am so sorry, but I do mind - only a few minutes, please? You might sleep better after a walk, and it is such a nice evening?"

"Capital idea!" Grandfather unwittingly comes to Geoffrey's aid. "A stroll in the garden will put roses on your cheeks!"

'Roses be damned!' I think in despair and plead, "Really, I'd rather not. Please, Geoffrey?"

"Of course, darling, let me take you to your room."

"Why don't you keep Grandfather company instead?" I suggest. "I am sure he would enjoy having his after-dinner port and pipe with both of you." I don't know why I have suggested that, but I kiss Grandfather and Geoffrey good-night before they have a chance to say anything and nod to Rupert who has settled down with the newspaper. He is the picture of absorbed interest, except for the fingers of one hand which drum restlessly against the arm of his chair! He knows ... I know he knows ... but how?

What I do next I cannot explain in words that would make sense to anybody, least of all me:

Instead of going upstairs I walk through the hall and run outside. I know it is irrational, the worst thing I could possibly do - but the need to get away from Rupert has pushed what little logical thinking I have left out of my head. I run around the house and down one of the paths that leads towards the sea. I run hard, as fast as I can, keep running, I don't care where, all the way to the rocks - and suddenly Rupert materializes from behind one of them! How can he already be there, when only minutes ago he was so engrossed in his newspaper? 'Seemed to be engrossed,' I remind myself, he must have left by one of the rear doors which is a much shorter way. How did he know?

Dear God, what have I done?

"Going somewhere, Cousin? Why don't we walk *this* way?"

Effortlessly, in one deft motion, he turns me around by twisting my arm and marches me towards the cliffs. I want to protest but cannot say anything, my chest feels raw from running so hard.

"Cat got your tongue, eh?" he sneers.

When I don't answer he stops walking and, without releasing his grip on my arm, looks me over and almost sadly, it seems, says, "Poor, poor, silly Aglaia."

I hate myself for my inability to react. Why can't I think of something? Something, anything to help me!

"I ... I don't know what you mean."

"You don't really think that I am such a fool, do you? You know exactly what I mean: You lied about when and how far you went riding, the other morning. How do I know? Easy. You didn't do very well getting the sand off your boots and the hem of your riding habit, that's how, especially in the back where I guess you cannot see; not off your horse, either! All of which points to one particular sandy cove - remember now? Of course you do. I know you've taken ThatsThat - what a ridiculous name for a horse - there before. *You were at the stables early, you must have overheard us; you rode off after we left.* The proof? You have not been yourself ever since that morning. How am I doing so far?" He ends with a self-congratulatory smirk.

"What are you talking about?" I am not going to admit to anything but how do I keep desperation out of my voice?

"Not convinced yet?"

I don't answer. A tiny hope has sprung up in my mind: he loves to brag, perhaps I can gain time if I let him talk - never mind that I don't know time for what.

"You might as well admit it, Cousin: you were there, you heard us, and that means that now you know things you are not supposed to know. Which is too, too bad. For you, that is," he adds with a nasty laugh; he is enjoying himself. "So isn't it too, too perfect that everyone thinks you are safe in your bed, dreaming sweet wedding dreams?"

He is so sure that he has thought of everything. In desperation I ask, "What did I ever do to you? Couldn't you let me go? I don't want anything, I'll leave, I'll go back to Brig, I won't say anything, I promise ..." As soon as I have said the words contempt pushes up inside and sickens me. How can I say that, how can I forget about Grandfather? "Why? In God's name why? I didn't come for the money!" I shout at him.

"Well, that may be so," he allows, all injured innocence, "but how was I to know that? By the way, don't bother shouting: we are quite alone here."

I ignore that. "How did you find me, I mean at the very beginning?" I had puzzled over that for so long: he knew that I was Aglaia Trelawney before I did. How? Through his friend, I now know, but answering will keep him talking. He will insist on telling me, I hope, in great detail.

He laughs. "Yes, that was an awful shock, learning that the old man has a granddaughter who lives with the cows in some God-forsaken mountain valley in Switzerland ... but of course you remember my friend Tony, Mr. Anthony Thornton to you - poor chap who was reduced to teaching you girls English?"

I shall have the confirmation I want *if* I can keep him talking. "Yes, I remember Mr. Thornton. What about him?"

"Well, Tony and I go back many years." Rupert seems delighted to explain. "Same boarding school, later London where the poor sod lost his shirt gambling. I, of course, raked it in, literally by the way. When Debtors' Prison threatens to become his next 'accommodation', being a loyal friend and all that, I help him to get out of England, and to disappear. Forgery is one of Tony's many talents; he creates glowing references and in no time is hired at a Geneva girls' school. Imagine his surprise when, one day, he walks into a classroom and what does he see dangling from a tender young neck? You guessed it, *the Trelawney locket!* Come to think of it, now is as good a time as any to relieve you of it!"

A second too late my hand flies to my neck. Rupert has already grabbed the chain. He rips it off my neck, dangles it from his hand and examines the broken catch. My shawl drops from my shoulders. "Of course Tony recognized the importance of this little trinket."

"Importance?" I hope I have managed the right amount of confusion.

"A little dense, Cousin, aren't you? Tony had been to the Manor many times before the old man decided he was 'persona non grata' - I assume you don't need a translation? Didn't think you would. By now even you must have noticed how many Trelawney ladies were painted wearing it. Ah, I see you are getting the picture. Hey, picture, that *is* clever!" He takes a moment to delight in his word play. "To get back to Tony: he lost no time informing me of his discovery. Neither did I - lose time, I mean. I ordered him to check into your past history. The rest, as they say, was child's play."

"What was child's play?" I don't have to act confused. I am confused.

Rupert looks at me with pity for my inability to grasp what he is explaining so brilliantly. "Finding out who you really are, of course! For one thing, my dear, you are so unmistakably, so damnably a Trelawney! Well, Tony owed me: I ordered him to arrange for you to leave school early; unfortunately I had to leave certain details up to him, such as how and when ..."

"Arrange?" The word bursts out of me. "Arrange what?"

"No need to shout, and no need either to pretend you don't understand! You know exactly what I mean."

"Yes, *now* I understand. You killed my father! Why? What did he ever do to you?"

"Now, now - how can you blame me when I was right here in Cornwall, slaving away in your grandfather's business?" Rupert answers reasonably. "As I said, I had to leave some details up to Tony and friends, and good Lord, did the twit make a shambles of it! He is even more inept than your Geoffrey! A poisoned chocolate drink - what a bloody, bloody stupid idea! Come to think of it, the only thing he got right was to get Geoffrey a seat on your coach!"

He had my Father killed. I picture how Tony and friends left him lying in the snow, helpless and injured, and there is such a wild rage in me that I want to throw myself at Rupert and beat him with my fists and kick him senseless and scratch his eyes out - but I need to keep him talking. What was that about a coach? Never mind. I can only think about Father ...

"But ... Mr. Thornton, where did he ...?" My thoughts are racing off in so many directions that I have no control over what I am saying.

"Where did he go when he left Geneva in such a rush - is that what you would like to know? So would I! Could be he is already 'one of the blest above', but - come to think of it - 'one of the blest below' seems much more likely, don't you agree, Cousin?"

I ignore that. "Why my father? Why? What did he ever do to you?"

Incredulous, he shakes his head. "How can you still not understand? *He saved your life, that's what he did!* Without you we have no problem. With you - do I have to spell it out? Didn't think so. You don't really expect me to let years of slaving away to get on the old man's good side go down the drain - or up in smoke, if you prefer? Why should I let you rob me of what is rightfully mine?"

"But Father ..." I weep. I have no weapons, nothing to fight against this madman's twisted logic.

"Oh, stop sniveling!" In vain I search for something, anything to say. I think I hear a noise and risk a glance in that direction.

"No point looking for help." Rupert's mocking laugh

reverberates among the rocks. "Geoffrey will not rush to your rescue! Sorry to disappoint you, cousin: having checked on his peacefully slumbering bride, he remains at the Manor. It is what I ordered him to do and to explain to Sir Arthur, provided he arrives, that you retired early, but that you are so looking forward to seeing him in the morning. Yes, your Geoffrey is staying put. He knows better than to disobey orders."

I am no match for him, he has thought of everything. It will be over soon: there is nothing left for me to ask, nothing left for him to explain. Strangely enough, the sense of helplessness is gone. What I am left with is fear, of course, fear - but also a rage greater than any I have ever felt and relief that there is no need any longer to hide what I think.

"Not that it will make the slightest difference to you," I scream, shaking with the intensity of my fury, "but before you do whatever you are planning in that sick, warped mind of yours, I shall have the satisfaction of telling you that you are the most despicable human being that ever walked the earth! No, I take that back: you are not human, you are less than human, and some day you will pay ... for what you did to my father, for what you tried to do to Grandfather, oh yes, I know about that! For what you are going to do to me, and for what you have undoubtedly done to others who've had the bad luck of getting in your way! You are monsters, both of you, monsters!" I stop shouting only because I have run out of breath.

Amusement flashes quickly over Rupert's face. "Temper, temper," he shakes his head, "I take the strongest exception to your accusations!" But in the blink of an eye his face turns an angry red. "How dare you! You need to be taught a lesson!" He steps closer and I try to squirm away, but before I know it he has me backed up against a large boulder with one arm and with his balled fist strikes a blow to the side of my head. It smashes against the rock. I am afraid I will fall down with the pain that radiates out from the back of my skull, but something in me commands, 'don't give up!' as he readies himself for another blow.

"Don't you dare!" Geoffrey's voice, furious, savage.

Rupert whips around without releasing his hold on me and I nearly fall. "What in bloody hell are you doing here?"

Geoffrey strikes away Rupert's arm before he can hit me again.

"I told you again and again: no violence!"

"And I told you again and again that I am bloody tired carrying you, you Goddamn lamebrain!"

Rupert tightens his grip on my arm. The ground shifts under my feet, I am being dragged towards the edge. Pulled backward, too? I understand: no weapon, nothing that would leave tell-tale marks - just a most unfortunate drowning ...

"*Aglaia!*"

I fight as hard as I can against being dragged forward, but my other arm is being pulled backwards at the same time with such force that I scream with the pain of it. I fear it will be torn from its socket. Geoffrey?

"You God-damn idiot!" Rupert screams. "Pull with me, Geoff, *not bloody against me! With me!*"

The sound of the sea grows to a loud roar as I brace myself against the push I know will come any second - half-thoughts form only to vanish again - Geoffrey is here he is trying to help me he called my name I knew he would come dear God let it be high tide if I can just avoid the rocks ... Simon ...

"What in bloody hell are you doing now?"

I am not being pulled backwards any more, Rupert's grip on my arm is loosened and I am shoved forward with tremendous force, far out over the cliff. For a second I think a dark shape hurtles past me and there is a cry, I don't know whether mine or Geoffrey's, and then only the shock of icy water swirling around me and the panic of being pulled down. Father's calm, reassuring voice, 'Don't struggle against the water, go with it, use your arms and legs, swim, don't panic. Swim, you know how.'

Yes, I know how. Arms and legs move - I have not slammed onto the rocks God only knows how that is possible I have a chance only a very small chance perhaps I can do this I am wearing a light summer dress and only one petticoat nothing heavy but it is pulling me pulling me down so strongly I am breathing did I remember to breathe before I went under think of the water churning around me as the lake in the mountains where I learned to swim very much against my mother's objections because there is no need for girls to know how to swim but this is no serene mountain lake this the angry ocean intent on drowning me - Father's voice has faded away - I hear myself think and speak to the buffeting waves slamming into me I mustn't let myself be dragged back out again why have I lost my boots because I wore the light short ones and never laced them up properly but that is good now I can try to curl my toes around sand and pebbles the roar of the waves is deafening it drives everything from my mind except the urge to save myself don't die don't die don't die and still the sucking swirling motion of the sea sweeps everything out from under my feet makes me scrabble for purchase so many times - until now! I gain a tiny bit of ground with one wave a little more on the next one enough with the one after that.

I drag myself against the cliff where I am sure I cannot be seen from above. Don't make a sound. Rupert's voice mingles with the cark, cark, cark of the screeching gulls which skim back and forth over the water.

"Answer me! Aglaia! Geoffrey! Answer me!"

I cannot stop shivering and my arm hurts. I remain pressed against the cliff, listen for Rupert calling our names. There is a last shout, a sob almost, "Geoffrey! Brother!" Then silence.

Geoffrey did go against his brother in the end, perhaps for the first time in his life and with no concern about the consequences to him. I know that. If he hadn't pushed me forward, so hard, I would have fallen on the rocks ... he did try to save me ... he did save me but too late, it was too late, too late for us. Where is he?

I realize that I am alone here ...

I wait as long as I dare. Rupert must be on his way back to the Manor which leaves me one choice: going in the opposite direction, towards the Wheal Lizzie cottages. It is far, and first I have to find the way to the top which I hope really is at the other end of this cove. Isn't that what Geoffrey told me once, a lifetime ago?

There are new pains when I get to my feet and try some steps. Cuts? I must have stepped on mussels or some other shells. The stinging sensation in my upper arm, I see, is from a bleeding cut, but not a very deep one; let's hope the salt water cleaned it. The back of my head hurts, and so do my feet, but I am alive. Alive.

I drag myself along the narrow spur of wet sand until, much later, I find the way up; in some places it is slippery with dark moss. When I reach the top, fatigue pulls me down like a heavy weight and I let myself fall against some bushes - only a few minutes, I promise myself. I am cold; the chill of the sea is seeping into my bones, but the fear of what Rupert will do next urges me back on my feet. What if he returns, and he will, with a rescue party no doubt! Sobbing, "I tried so desperately to reach her, but she fell ... and my poor, poor brother did, too, trying to save her!" The evil low miserable abominable despicable lying conniving unscrupulous fiend ...

Anger floods back into me. I flex my cold-stiff fingers until they bend and I can pull the soaked fichu off my neck; I wring it out and manage to wrap it around my arm. That takes some time, so does getting to my feet. There is nothing I can do about my sore shoulder. I set out, wishing it were with more hope, more bravery.

It is windy, dark clouds race across the sky, but there is a three-quarter moon. I'll be all right. It has to be. I have ridden this way many times, all I have to do is keep the sea to my right until the path turns inland ... I wish I was sitting astride ThatsThat – how can feet hurt and go numb at the same time? Thin stockings are not much good for walking and stumbling around, but that's all I have, no use moaning about it. I keep going. My clammy clothing stiffens and chafes as the saltwater in it dries. Cold, cold ... keep going ... I stumble ... keep going ...

The next thing I see, much, much later is a light, very

far away. Go towards the light, go. I count steps, lose track of counting, the light comes closer, no it doesn't, lights don't move, I'm the one who is doing the moving but slowly, so very slowly ... and then I fall against a door, which opens, seemingly all by itself.

Chapter XVIII

The room spins around - but perhaps I am doing the spinning?

Someone says my name, again and again.

I want to reach for something to steady myself, but one of my arms doesn't move very well, a sharp pain shoots through my shoulder. I open my eyes - too bright. Maybe slow breaths will make the dizziness go away. No, that doesn't feel right either.

I must have made a sound - there is a gentle touch on my forehead. The coolness of a compress. A sip of water. A soothing voice. I sleep again and dream. Nightmares in which I tumble from great heights into darkness.

There is a presence which makes the nightmares go away, someone who restrains me when I fight to get out of bed, who does things to my shoulder and my arm and my feet, who raises me up to take sips of water or tea or soup, who never leaves.

Sometimes, when I surface into consciousness, I think I recognize the voice, but I must be wrong. Wrong or dreaming ...

When I wake up, really wake up, the dizziness is gone. Little by little the room straightens itself out, my eyes travel over familiar furniture and objects and I cry out in panic: I am in my room, I am back at the Manor! The nightmare is not over.

"Hush, Aglaia, hush, you are safe, everything is all right." The voice is Simon's and comes from over by the window, but that is impossible. Simon is in Brig. Or I am still dreaming ... I hear the familiar shuffle as he approaches my bed.

"Simon?" I attempt to raise myself on one elbow, but the movement hurts my shoulder and makes my head throb.

He nods and makes me lie down again. "Welcome back. You've taken your sweet time waking up and gave everybody quite a scare! Everything is all right, Aglaia, everything is all right."

"Simon, you are *here*?" He looks as if he hadn't slept in a very long time.

"Certainly looks that way, doesn't it?"

"But ... but how?"

"The usual way - coach, train, steamer, more coaches ..."

"No, I don't mean that!"

"I know, I know. Terrible joke, worse timing. I apologize." He pulls a chair over to my bed and sits down. "Go back to sleep. We'll talk again later ... soon."

I fall asleep again, a deep, good sleep this time, and when I wake up, Simon is here, asking questions - no, I do not feel dizzy any longer; no, the back of my head does not hurt, well, only when I touch the bandage, did they have to shave much of my hair? All right, I won't touch it and yes, of course I know that hair grows back; no, there is no pain when I breathe; yes, my shoulder and my arm are still sore, and so are the bottoms of my feet; no, that is all; no, no other aches and pains - don't you think that's enough for *one* person?

"She is feeling better," Simon says to the room, then he turns towards me. "Questions?"

Do I have questions, lots of them! I am wondering how and where to begin when he says, "Why don't I tell you everything from my end, so to speak, and then you ask away?"

I nod, relieved that he is making it so easy for me.

"All right, then, from the beginning. Well, the invitation to your wedding arrived and I was crushed ..."

I look up at him. This wouldn't be another one of his badly timed jokes? I see that it isn't.

"Olga, needless to say, goes into one of her dithers," he continues. "How would we travel, how long would it take? When she finds out that it means coaches, plural, a ship across the English Channel (yes, a bit wider than Lake Geneva, I think) and after that more coaches or one of them "fangled" trains (you remember she always skips 'new'-) ... I am sure you can picture her as she crosses herself, calls on all Saints but especially her Saint Jadwiga and says, sobbing, "You know I be lovin' that girl so so much, but all them trains, ships, coaches? Too many, too many."

Yes, that is exactly how I pictured Olga's reaction.

"What about you?"

Simon looks squarely at me. "I've had more than enough time to think about this and everything else. Talked to Olga a few times, too - amazing how the woman cuts through nonsense and gets at the truth in no time! Well, I decided that I have to tell you the truth." He pauses for a moment. "So here it is: I was too jealous to come."

"Jealous?"

"Jealous, confused, devastated, fighting angry - all of the above and then some - but especially jealous. What could I do but send regrets? Of course Olga knew, I don't know how, but she has known all along. Told both of us once, she reminded me. So one day she stands before me, won't let me pass and says, "Time for talk plain, Doctor. You no good for nobody now, told you oncest you blind, both yous. How much longer you not understand? Go! Go see her! Is simple. I go pack." She marches away, grumbling loudly enough to make sure I hear every single word: "*Book-smart folk, sometime they be so people-stupid!*" She is right about that, about many other things, too! I understand that I have to go to Cornwall, wherever or whatever that is, if only to see with my own eyes that you are well and happy. I arrange for a colleague to take over during my absence, but there was also the not so small matter of your wedding present - although, strictly speaking, can I make you a present of something you already own?"

This is too much for me to comprehend, never mind answer. I am still back in that other part, the one when he said he was jealous. Jealous, does that mean what I am beginning to think it means?

"Well, the explanation about the present can wait until later," Simon adds unhelpfully, "but it did make for some unusual transportation problems. Anyway, at last I make it to a place called Mill Brook, at the same time as another guest, a Sir Arthur Harrington. We have barely stepped down from our coaches when a frantic youngster by the name of Benjamin races towards us and pulls at him, hands him letter from you and, sobbing, shouts an incoherent tale at him that you are in danger at the Manor. The gentleman immediately arranges for the constabulary to be notified and orders two horses to be saddled up for us. Don't ask how he manages all that within minutes or how much it cost - all was arranged with incredible dispatch. Benjamin and I take off like a couple of madmen, with Sir Arthur and the present following - Aglaia, are you up to hearing the rest?"

"Don't you dare stop!" I threaten, and it feels so right to be laughing together.

"Very well, then. We arrive at the Manor and are told that you have retired for the night. Under the circumstances that doesn't make sense - surely you would have waited for Sir Arthur's arrival. My bag is always with me, so, citing doctor's privileges, I announce that I am going to look in on you. I cannot tell you what goes through my head when you are not in your room - and when we learn that Rupert is not at the Manor either! Sir Arthur had told me that after reading your letter he was convinced that Rupert is behind whatever foul play is being planned or, God forbid, has already been set in motion. I keep praying that you are not where he is ..."

Only seconds ago we were laughing together - reliving these awful moments Simon looks so devastated I want to say something, but he shakes his head. "Let me finish - somebody remembers that there had been talk about you and Geoffrey going for a stroll in the gardens. By now I am also very concerned about your grandfather who is so worried about you, so agitated that he has trouble breathing.

"*Go find her! You must find her!*" he keeps shouting at me. I have only enough time to ask the butler to stay with him before we hurry outside. I curse loudly when I see the size of those gardens, how are we ever going to find you in there? Benjamin races ahead, we shout your name, look everywhere. Nothing. Going back we nearly collide with a wild-looking, disheveled 'gentleman' ..."

"Rupert?"

"Rupert!" Simon repeats, angrier than I have ever seen him, "clutching what turns out to be your shawl in his hands. He seems shaken when he sees us but recovers quickly. He tells us that there has been the most dreadful accident at the cliffs. You slipped - he doesn't know how it happened, he says, and in trying to save you, poor Geoffrey also fell. He says he kept calling your names for a long time, but he fears that both of you may have been injured in the fall ... and that you must have drowned. Of course he doesn't explain what *he* was doing there, but he weeps! Rivers, oceans of tears! You cannot imagine how distraught he *seems* to be: he weeps into your shawl, but I catch him watching for our reactions and then 'adjusting' the flow of his tears!"

"That does not surprise me, not in the least! And then?"

"We are not wasting another second with him even though he shouts after us, "You're too late, you're too late!" Benjamin runs off in the direction Rupert had appeared from, we follow as quickly as we can. When we reach an area where you must have been standing, Barry - well he goes berserk, there is no other way to describe it and ...."

"You brought Barry to me?" I shout, sitting up too quickly, "where is he?"

Simon makes me lie down again. "Outside I would think, with Benjamin *sitting on him*. Because he - Barry, not Benjamin - tries to jump onto your bed every time I let him into your room. Obviously not a good idea ... Now where was I? Oh yes, Barry must have picked up your scent; he runs to the cliff edge, circles, runs back again," ... the anguish in his eyes says more than his words. "We look down, of course, but see nothing but water crashing over the rocks and there's no way down, as far as we can see. Benjamin crawls around on all fours, sees something glistening in the grass - your locket, still on its chain. He bursts into tears. I am wild with despair and so is Sir Arthur, needless to say in a more gentlemanly and more sedate manner. Suddenly Barry takes off as if shot from a cannon! We follow as fast as we can. When we reach him he sniffs around some bushes. Suddenly he stops, stands still for a second, then he seems hell-bent on racing down a path that leads inland. Sir Arthur wants to have the police brought in to search all the areas down below, but I'm watching your dog: he barks, runs ahead and back again, circles around, nudges and pushes at me, whines, tries to pull me by my trouser leg, barks - he is showing us which way to go and is getting aggravated at how slowly we humans react to dog-hints. He races off. Fortunately, I am able to convince Sir Arthur and we follow him."

I am still smiling about the dog-hints but manage to ask, "But where did you find me?"

"You don't remember?"

"Well, I remember trying to get to the miners' cottages, but they were so far away ..."

"They were, they are. I don't know how you managed on your poor feet, but you did get there. Barry stops at a cottage; he howls and barks, attacks the door and scares the woman who finally opens it a crack nearly out of her wits. I don't understand one word she says, but Sir Arthur does, at least a good part of it: she says she found the 'Angel Lady' - meaning you - and took you inside, tried to wash sand and dirt off your legs and feet before she put you on a bed and covered you with one of your blankets. While he tries to convince her that we mean you no harm, that we are your friends I tell Benjamin to take Barry away from the door and to *keep him away*. Then I point to myself and say the word 'doctor' in every language I can think of - Arzt, physician, docteur, dottore, médecin and that I need to look at your injuries. Poor woman keeps shaking her head at me and won't let us in. That's when Sir Arthur bellows, and I mean bellows, "For pity's sake, man, do you really think people here understand French or German or Italian? Use your bloody head and show her your bloody bag, and do it bloody now!"

"Sir Arthur said that - he said bloody?" I cannot believe it.

"He did - three times!" Simon nods emphatically. "Greatly surprised himself, I think. Well, my bag did the trick, she let us in, and the rest you know. We brought you back here where you could be properly cared for. You were a very sick girl and gave us quite a scare."

"Was it you who took care of me?"

"You don't think I'd let anyone else near you?" Suddenly he looks the happiest I have ever seen him look. "Especially after you kept saying my name. Oh yes, you did, Aglaia, many, many times. Of course you were running a fever then, but ..."

"I was? I did?" I don't remember. I think I am blushing, but I am happy, so happy. And I am very clear in my mind that saying his name had nothing to do with a fever, nothing at all.

But a new fear grips me. "Grandfather - how is he?"

Simon doesn't answer right away and I fear the worst. Taking my hand he says, "He had a stroke later that night. I imagine that the shock of nearly losing you, learning that at least one of his nephews was a dangerous crook; finding out how cruelly both had used him, but especially you - *you* are his only concern in this - it may have been too much for him. I believe he is alive only because he waits to see you. I report to him every day and he understands that you are recovering; I wish I could tell you that he will, too ... but I don't see that happening. I wish I did. I am sorry, Aglaia, so very sorry."

I lean back into my pillows, exhausted and sad, but happy, too.

"Yes, rest now," Simon orders. "Besides, I don't have another dry handkerchief." Smiling, he takes the sodden one out of my hand.

I grab his sleeve. "No, Simon, wait! I have to know - what about Rupert? Where is he?"

"I wish we knew. Of course he was long gone when we arrived back at the Manor. Apparently having stopped there just long enough to help himself to money from your grandfather's safe - but don't worry, he was too smart to take the ring! There are warrants out for his arrest and that of his accomplices. Sir Arthur took care of everything and that includes seeing that theft is added to the other charges, and also putting up a very generous reward. As far as I know the authorities have not caught up any of them yet, but they will. And in case you don't already know: *you* are the one with all the friends around here, not Rupert!"

There is one more question I must ask. "Geoffrey?"

Simon's eyes never leave my face when he tells me

that Geoffrey's body was washed ashore several miles north of here, three days after the 'accident'. "I went with Benjamin who identified him. His injuries lead me to believe that it may have been over quickly - I cannot be sure, of course, but I hope I'm right. And that is absolutely, definitively all for now." He pulls the covers up around me. "I'll be back soon, and then we'll talk again." Very gently his hand caresses my cheek.

Feeling drowsy and at peace I look up into his face and wonder why I have never seen what I am seen so clearly now.

"Simon ..."

"Tomorrow," he touches a finger from his lips to mine. "Tomorrow."

Chapter XIX

Many tomorrows have come and gone since that day, and much that I did not understand has become clearer in my mind.

Simon and I talked for hours. During these long conversations the many misunderstandings that clouded and came close to destroying what we felt for one another, during Father's illness and afterwards - once explained and understood, they ceased to matter.

Now I understand Simon's reaction when I came home from Geneva that spring - he says that is when he stopped thinking about me in what he calls 'a brotherly way' and realized he was falling in love with me. I understand what his fear could do to him, his carefully hidden fear that I might not care 'for a lame man who had so little to offer.' But that is when I shout 'stop!' and tell him never to use the word 'lame' again, that as a doctor/ dottore/médecin/Arzt etc. etc. he ought to know better: he walks with a slight limp, that's all, and as far as having 'so little to offer' - doesn't he know me better than that?

He explains how that fear turned into resignation when he discovered that Father's will had left me well-off, and how that resignation became hopelessness when I told him about my new identity. We promise each other never to let silence come between us again.

Knowing that sooner or later I was going to worry about this, he also tells me that all the guests had been notified by telegraph that the wedding was canceled. Not all were reached in time, but all expressed relief that I was recovering from my ordeal; more than a few pronounced my survival nothing short of miraculous. I know it was. "You have stacks of letters to answer," he adds helpfully.

After that he says it is my turn.

Looking very serious, he says he needs to know whether I truly loved Geoffrey, loved him enough to marry him, whether I still do and whether I am still grieving for him. He asks me to hold nothing back and to be totally, totally honest.

I have thought about this for a long, long time.

I think in the beginning I was simply flattered; no dashing young man had ever paid attention to me before. Geoffrey came along at a time when I didn't know what to do with myself, about myself, my life, when I was unsure of everything - he was engaging, solicitous, good company, and he did fall in love with me, whether 'ordered to' by his brother or not! And I? I just let it all happen, it felt right, it felt good - it was easy to blind myself to what I didn't want to see, to believe only what I wanted to believe. That is the uncomfortable truth I've had to confront. Would Geoffrey have loved me had I not been Aglaia Trelawney? I'll never know. All I know is that everything happened *because* that is who I am.

Once I understood that traveling to Paris in the same coach was one of many carefully contrived 'coincidences', that his 'delighted surprise' in finding me at the Manor and his talk about fate was an accomplished piece of acting, I had to face that he had lied to me from the very beginning. But I never doubted that, within weeks, he came to love me; I don't doubt it now. When he did go against his brother in the end, he was someone I had never truly known, someone I could not respect or love.

Did I grieve for him? I am sad that he died the way he did, in pain and alone, never knowing that he saved me with the strong shove that carried me farther out, away from the rocks - but from the beginning I told myself that it was better this way. I don't think of him as a criminal; if captured, he would be jailed with felons and I don't know how he could have survived that. I am not greatly surprised that Sir Arthur does not share my thinking. The fact that Geoffrey was told of Rupert's schemes only *after* the fact carries no weight with him; to him he remains a willing accomplice. I owe Sir Arthur a great deal and will always be grateful and fond of him, but he is a very stern judge!

I still don't know why I didn't want to see the weakness in Geoffrey, that complete dependence of his on Rupert. Perhaps I saw only what I wanted to see, believed only what I wanted to believe ... haven't I said that before? I did learn that it is not enough to say 'I don't want to have anything to do with violence'. That is merely closing your eyes to something you know to be wrong.

Perhaps it has much to do with feeling lost and alone after Father died, with reading his notebook and trying to understand a world that had been turned upside down. I did like Geoffrey from the start - and I tell Simon that I know I am repeating myself, and that I don't know whether any of this makes sense to him - and that there is something else I should also tell him, but that I don't know how to go about it ...

Simon looks at me for some long moments before he smiles and says, "Aglaia, there is nothing in this whole world that you have to worry about telling me, ever. Tell me now if you want to, or tell me in an hour, tomorrow, next month, next year, twenty years from now - we have all the time in the world."

Well, this goes back a few years, but what I am thinking is this: Veronica and Ingrid used to brag to us younger girls about their experiences with their beaus, saying, among other pearls of wisdom, "Oh, you'll know it is the real thing when you feel all shimmery inside when he kisses you!" I was much too embarrassed to admit that I had no idea what they were talking about, but Monique, always the literally-minded realist, spoke up and pointed out that shimmery not only wasn't a proper word but wasn't in her dictionary. Trying unsuccessfully to suppress their giggles, the twins answered, "When it happens to you you'll know that it is the *perfect* word, and you won't do research in a silly dictionary anymore!"

Of course I don't say it in those words, I couldn't ... but Simon said to be totally honest, and I want to get this over with, out of the way ... so, keeping my eyes on the coverlet and tracing its leafy design with a finger, I haltingly admit that I used to wonder whether there shouldn't be more than sweetness when Geoffrey kissed me, something different? I don't want to blush, but I feel that tell-tale red warmth creeping up over my throat and my face and I am so embarrassed that I don't know what to do - except to dive under the covers. Oh God, what is Simon going to make of this?

What he does is he uncovers my face, bends down and cups my face with his hands. His kiss starts out sweet, lingers ... and ...

"Sweet?" he inquires, releasing me.

When I get my breath back, I manage, "N-no, shimmery!" and pull him to me again. For an instant, he looks perplexed, but then a knowing smile spreads over his face. In a husky voice he murmurs something I don't quite understand because it turns into another kiss.

He remains at the Manor until he is satisfied that I am fully recovered which coincides perfectly with receiving official notification that Rupert, Mr. Thornton and two accomplices have been apprehended and are behind bars.

So yes, I am still at Trelawney Manor.

I cannot leave while Grandfather is alive. He knows when I am with him and of course I do most of the talking. Sometimes it is difficult to understand him; at other times, when he tries very hard, he manages a a few words that I understand and I guess at the others.

His bedroom is above the music room. I have had the piano moved as close to the window as possible. On mild afternoons, with the upstairs and downstairs windows wide open, I play my 'Song without Words' for him, twice in a row and, with apologies to Felix Mendelssohn, *fortissimo* from beginning to end to make sure that the sound travels up to him! When I am done I rush back up to his room: sometimes the smile is more in his eyes than on his lips, but he always manages a 'thank-you', or he simply repeats 'dear girl, dear girl.'

I keep telling him that Trelawneys will be living here after him and me; that calms and pleases him. Sometimes he asks to hold the locket - I like to think that it brings back good memories to him. When he asks, "Ring?" I assure him that it is where it belongs, in his safe. He insists that the miniatures are mine to keep.

One afternoon some weeks later, Stratton asks permission to remain in Grandfather's room. "I shall sit quietly in a corner, Miss Aglaia, you will never know am here. It is only in case I am needed." I ask him to move his chair next to mine. I sense more than understand why he needs to be here.

Shortly before it gets dark, Grandfather indicates with his chin and by opening his good hand that he wants me to move closer. "Dear girl ... tired."

I take his hand in mine. "That's all right, Grandfather, there's no need to talk. I'm happy just sitting here with you." He falls asleep.

I watch him, lost in my thoughts about all that has happened here in the past two years, and I am pretty sure Stratton goes over old times too, about the many decades he has lived here and been with Grandfather. Barry is dozing at my feet.

Grandfather awakes more than an hour later. He looks at me with the piercing glance that used to be so much part of him. "Aglaia," he says, with great effort but quite clearly. "Aglaia, n-name ... n-name is ... Tamsyn ... Penwarne ... Tamsyn." I know he had to summon all the will and strength that was left in him to say this.

"My mother's name was Tamsyn Penwarne?" I repeat, weeping, holding on to his hand with both of mine. He nods yes, looks at me, then his eyes close. My mother's name is his last gift to me, the most precious one he had to give, the most difficult.

A little later Stratton whispers to me that Tamsyn is an old Cornish diminutive for Thomasina.

We are both with Grandfather when he dies in his sleep later that evening.

I have had a great many things to think about and many decisions to make. I am not sure that I am going to try to find my mother's family. For obvious reasons I would not approach another search in the same manner, but I might ask Sir Arthur to look into this at some future time. Not now - all I can think of now is going home.

Building is making progress on new cottages where the old ones proved to be beyond repair, and not only at Wheal Lizzie. They will be leased to the miners for a token rent, a step that does not endear me to some of the mine owners, but so be it. Others, I am happy to learn, are beginning to see the need for change.

Sir Arthur is charged with exploring who is next in line to inherit the Trelawney holdings. There are several sons among the Ceylon tea growers branch, two of whom are considering a change of place and occupation. Two sons - that would have pleased Grandfather! While we await the outcome off this search, the ring remains here in the safe; it is to be given to the descendant, if and when he returns to Cornwall, so that one part of the family tradition may continue.

It this should fail to come about, everything will be sold, at auction, I suppose. Stratton and the rest of the staff are to receive generous pensions, regardless whether they remain with a new owner or not. The new owner will be bound by contract to honor the miners' rental arrangements and to assure Benjamin of a home and position as groom for as long as he wants - he gets along well with the other stable lads and hopes to move up head groom, " 'orses bein' ever so much better 'n school; ain't nowt better 'n animals, innit, Miss?" is the way he still likes to put it. I know he will take good care of ThatsThat.

For the time being, he will be travelling to London with me and Barry. Sir Arthur has been in frequent contact with Simon. They have engaged in extensive back-and-forth correspondence regarding the transport of 160 pounds of Saint Bernard through England, across the Channel and into and through France, into Switzerland, and lastly up to Brig. Naturally, Simon considers himself an expert.

Apparently Sir Arthur has also told Simon that taking care of my affairs has involved him in more adventures than he ever took part in during his long but not overly exciting legal career! He admitted that he had prided himself on *never* losing his temper and never swearing

- except for a certain evening in a miners' cottage when circumstances compelled him to raise his voice considerably above its customary level and he had to resort to exceptionally strong language.

I still wish I could have heard him say 'bloody' three times!

And now, that all of this has been taken care of and all the good-byes have been said Benjamin, Barry and I are on our way to London where Sir Arthur will join us. He looks forward to the long overdue visit with his good friend Kaspar, and I will get a chance to show Benjamin that there really *are* some mountains which never lose all their snow in summer. The two will travel back to England together.

In a few days we shall be home where, Simon wrote in his last letter - he writes very often now! - Olga is preparing to bake enough tortas to gladden the hearts of all the people in Brig.

Home, where Simon is waiting for me - and where one doctor in the family is enough, for the time being!

* * * * * * * * * * * * * *

Author's Note:

I have taken liberties with Swiss, French and English geography, but there really was a Nadezha Suvlova (1843-1918).

Her father, Prokofiy Suvlov, was a serf who worked as assistant estate manager for Prince Sheremetev, a member of one of Russia's wealthiest families. Suvlov's oldest and gifted daughters, Appolonia (always called Polina) and Nadezha, came to the Prince's attention; he arranged and paid for them to continue their education at a Moscow boarding school where they concentrated on science and foreign languages. Following this, Nadezha audited medical classes at the Saint Petersburg Medical School and passed the midwife exam. For some time she worked in physician and chemist Alexander Borodin's (1833-1887) laboratory; today Borodin is known as the composer of "In the Steppes of Central Asia" and his only opera "Prince Igor" rather than as physician.

After Russia banned women from university studies, Nadezha in 1866 became the first female accepted as medical student at a European university, Zürich University. Only one year later she received her degree in surgery/obstetrics. She returned to Russia and moved to the Crimea where she cared for the women of a nomadic Sunni Moslem tribe, the practice of her specialty being forbidden to their men.

Meanwhile her sister Polina, a writer, had met Fjodor Dostojewski (1821-1881) who was married and her senior by twenty years. She became his life-long mistress and is said to be the prototype for several female characters in his novels.

CPSIA information can be obtained at www.ICGtesting.com
Printed in the USA
BVOW08s0608240316

441449BV00001B/99/P